"No, let go!" She took a qu[...] a hand over her mouth. She[...] to wrench herself from his grasp as she aimed a frantic kick at his legs. Her toe rapped his shin.

"Ouch!" the man groaned. "Stop it, will you!"

Kim froze for a moment.

No, it couldn't be.

Once more she tried to break free, jabbing in the direction of his ribs with her elbows. Connection again.

"I said stop it!" he growled, jerking her closer. "I'm not going to—ow!"

Kim released a lungful of air, then took another deep breath as amazement consumed her. That voice, the size of him, even the fragrance, were all too familiar. Painfully familiar. But how could it possibly be? Just a few minutes ago she'd been thinking. . .

"Adam?" she ventured in a tiny voice.

The hard arm tautened around her. He stood, unmoving, for a full five seconds before the pressure of his grip eased.

A long silence stretched. "Tell me I'm hallucinating," a voice finally drawled, his Ozark accent unchanged by time, his voice even deeper than it used to be.

Kim nearly fell over with relief when he let her go. "Adam, it really is you!" She strained to see his dark, wavy hair and deep green eyes through the dark gray dawn. She caught only shadows, but it was him; there was no doubt. "I can't believe it!" Impulsively, she reached up to hug him. "I was just thinking about you, wondering if you ever came up here. . .anymore."

His whole body had stiffened. He did not return the hug. Kim fought a surprisingly strong wave of disappointment as she released him.

"Sorry, Adam, I was just so happy to see you again. I've never stopped thinking about you and your family, and I was hoping we could. . .you know. . .get together and talk about everything."

HANNAH ALEXANDER is the pen name for a husband and wife writing team from Missouri. Melvin works as a doctor while Cheryl writes full time. They are very active in their local church and mission projects.

Books by Hannah Alexander

HEARTSONG PRESENTS
HP274—The Healing Promise

Ozark
Sunrise

Hannah Alexander

Heartsong Presents

A note from the author:
*I love to hear from my readers! You may correspond with me
by writing:* **Hannah Alexander**
Author Relations
PO Box 719
Uhrichsville, OH 44683

ISBN 1-57748-617-X

OZARK SUNRISE

Cover design by Robyn Martins.

one

A bright, three-quarter moon highlighted the thick tree line where frog song echoed across the property of Sunrise Retreat, a Christian youth camp secluded in the Missouri Ozarks near Branson. The glow caressed the outline of one particular cabin, sending a shaft of light through an uncurtained window.

Kimberly Bryant turned over in her bed and tentatively smiled at the moonlight. She was back. It felt good. . .yet strange, almost frightening. After years of wandering, she was back at the camp where she had spent so much time as a kid.

This time she was going to be a counselor for girls who were just like she had been in her "wandering years." In the excitement, she couldn't close her eyes and go back to sleep.

Five minutes later, dressed in her jogging suit and shoes, her waist-length, golden-red hair hanging loose for warmth, she left the cabin. She always did her running in the morning before sunrise, loving the peace and silence that hovered in the air before anyone else stirred. Even in her home in Branson, where the tourist crowds had overrun the home folk, she still felt safe on the dark streets.

Kimberly's eyes gradually adjusted to the darkness, and she saw the other cabins clearly. Melancholy touched her for just a second when she glimpsed the outline of the camp chapel. She and her closest friends, Pam and Adam, had worshiped together often in that chapel when they were growing up, back when life was simpler—when her mom and dad were still alive—and Kim hadn't felt the weight and worry of life pressing down on her.

Kim knew she would be seeing her old friend Pam Reed

sometime today. She looked forward to it, glad she had made contact with Pam again.

Did Adam Patterson still visit here? More important, had he and his parents forgiven her for rejecting their comfortable home? Maybe they couldn't forgive her. When Kim's parents were killed in a car wreck six years ago, she'd had no relatives to take her in. The Pattersons, close friends of the family, had opened not only their home to her, but their hearts as well, welcoming her as the daughter they'd never had. A year later, at seventeen, still filled with bitterness at God and a deep loneliness, Kim had left the Patterson home in Eureka Springs, Arkansas. She knew it must have hurt them deeply.

The trees gave way to a wider hiking trail, and Kim increased her pace, jogging slowly to warm up. The peace of the forest surrounded her, and she smiled to herself, inhaling the sweet, clean air. It was good to be back, in spite of what might lie ahead these next six weeks. Once, this place had felt like her second home. Sometimes her parents used to bring her up here even when camp was not in session. The memory of those times was what had brought her here early, so she could spend the night alone before her campers arrived. If she had her choice of jobs, she would choose one right here, where she would never have to leave the peace of these hills and hollows again.

Deep in thought, Kim was startled by the flash of headlights reflected in the trees to her right. She scrambled off the trail before she realized that the car was traveling a dirt road parallel to the trail, separated by a thick stand of woods.

Artificial light illumined the woods as tires crunched twigs and pine cones. Curious about who would be driving up here this early in the morning, so far from any daily human activity, Kim tried to catch a glimpse of the automobile as it passed, but the tangle of undergrowth was too thick.

She was trying to find an easy way to plow through the

dense brush, when the car's headlights went out. Oddly. . .the car kept moving forward, slowly, stealthily.

Kim felt a rush of suspicion. This was Sunrise Retreat land, all two thousand acres of it. What was going on here?

Without thinking past her curiosity, she darted back onto the trail and jogged, easily keeping pace with the car. As she ran, the eastern sky barely lightened with predawn gray. One thing she didn't want to do was allow the people in that car to see her. She would have to be careful to stay—

"Oomph!" She collided with an unexpected barrier. She cried out in shock as she bounced backward. . .from a very pliable tree.

No, not a tree. It was a man. He reached toward her. With a gasp of horror, she whipped around to escape. The man grabbed her arms and held her firmly.

"No, let go!" She took a quick breath to scream. He clamped a hand over her mouth. She struck out with her hands, trying to wrench herself from his grasp as she aimed a frantic kick at his legs. Her toe rapped his shin.

"Ouch!" the man groaned. "Stop it, will you!"

Kim froze for a moment.

No, it couldn't be.

Once more she tried to break free, jabbing in the direction of his ribs with her elbows. Connection again.

"I said stop it!" he growled, jerking her closer. "I'm not going to—ow!"

Kim released a lungful of air, then took another deep breath as amazement consumed her. That voice, the size of him, even the fragrance, were all too familiar. Painfully familiar. But how could it possibly be? Just a few minutes ago she'd been thinking. . .

"Adam?" she ventured in a tiny voice.

The hard arm tautened around her. He stood, unmoving, for a full five seconds before the pressure of his grip eased.

A long silence stretched. "Tell me I'm hallucinating," a

voice finally drawled, his Ozark accent unchanged by time, his voice even deeper than it used to be.

Kim nearly fell over with relief when he let her go. "Adam, it really is you!" She strained to see his dark, wavy hair and deep green eyes through the dark gray dawn. She caught only shadows, but it was him; there was no doubt. "I can't believe it!" Impulsively, she reached up to hug him. "I was just thinking about you, wondering if you ever came up here. . .anymore."

His whole body had stiffened. He did not return the hug. Kim fought a surprisingly strong wave of disappointment as she released him.

"Sorry, Adam, I was just so happy to see you again. I've never stopped thinking about you and your family, and I was hoping we could. . .you know. . .get together and talk about everything. I know it's sudden, but I'm living back in Branson now, and I had the chance to—"

"Kim—"

"—come and work with girls who are going through some of the same—"

"Kim!" He grasped her shoulder and shook her gently. "I know. I'm helping with camp this year." He turned and looked in the direction the car had gone, then looked back at her. "Meeting someone?"

Kim stared at him, puzzled for a moment. "What? You mean the car? Of course not! I got up early to run. I don't know what that car was doing down here at this hour. They didn't even have their headlights on."

He hesitated, as if weighing her words. "Running in the dark is a dumb idea. You could bust an ankle on this trail if you can't see clearly."

No word of welcome, no warmth in his voice. In fact, he sounded almost as suspicious of her as she had been of the car.

Where was the old Adam, the comfortable buddy she had grown up with, shared with, treated like an older brother?

"So what are *you* doing down here in the dark?" she asked.

"Keeping an eye on things." Had she not known that voice so well, she would have thought it was the cold voice of a stranger, uncaring, unconcerned.

"You're still mad," she said. "Don't tell me you've held a grudge for five years! Come on, Adam, give me a break. I'm sorry, okay? It was awful of me, but I'm not like that now. Everything's—"

"We'll talk about it later." Adam glanced back toward the car. "Let's get back to camp." He walked in the direction Kim had come, not waiting to see if she followed.

For a moment, her old, rebellious spirit caught her in its grip. She wanted to refuse to go with him. What right did he have to treat her like he did, then calmly issue an order for her to follow?

Common sense won, however. Adam and the rest of his family had good reason to be reserved toward her, at least until they realized she had changed. She wasn't the same confused, unhappy kid who had struck out on her own five years ago.

"Adam, wait!" She rushed forward to walk alongside him. "You said you're helping with the camp this year? What position? Are you preaching now? You finished seminary a couple of years ago, didn't you?"

His steps slowed for a moment as he glanced at her in the growing light. She caught a telltale sign of white teeth when he smiled. It was brief. Too brief. Guarded.

"Still a chatterbox," he muttered. "Yes, I'm helping as assistant to the interim director, yes, I occasionally preach, and yes, I finished seminary two and a half years ago."

"You're probably wondering how I knew," she said. "I've kept up with the family. . .you know. . .you and John and Kate." She gave a defensive shrug. "I missed you, and I wanted to make sure you were okay, so I checked in with old friends in Eureka Springs. I found out that Clem Elliott got married, and his wife, Enid, adopted his daughter, Dani."

For a moment, Adam didn't speak. When he did, he slowed

his steps. "Yes, I know. They would have loved to have invited you to the wedding, but no one could find you. We got word of you from time to time. Mom and Dad wanted to try to contact you, but you never told anyone where you were. You didn't ever check with us. You didn't stop to think how worried we would be." He paused. "How hurt we would be." He shook his head and picked up his pace.

In spite of her long legs and good physical condition, Kim had trouble keeping up. Adam acted as if his treadmill had just switched into high gear.

Still, she felt a need to talk. "I didn't figure you would be too interested in hearing from me after all that. . .well, after I left, after all the trouble I gave you. Besides, five years is a long time, and I thought maybe life was a little more comfortable for everyone without me in it."

She waited, but he didn't make an effort to refute her words.

She glared at him, and if he had bothered to look, he'd have seen it clearly because the sky was turning brighter moment by moment. "Obviously I was right," she snapped.

Adam stopped abruptly with a deep sigh. The force of Kim's forward momentum carried her a few steps farther before she stopped and turned back.

She glimpsed the expression in the solid, unnaturally grim planes of his face. She saw no signs of the old, familiar warmth in his eyes, the indentations that, in a less masculine face, would be called dimples. In all the years she had known Adam, had been the closest of friends with him, she had never caught a glimpse of the coldness she saw there now. Their kindred spirits might never have been.

"You're wrong, Kim. How could you have lived with us that whole year—how could you have known us your whole life—and not know any of us any better than that?" The coldness suddenly hinted at a buried sense of betrayal. "How could you just go away and never tell any of us where you were? Do you know how much Mom and Dad grieved over you? How they prayed for you? And if you really did change, why didn't you get in touch with them—with us—then?"

Kim swallowed hard to find her voice. "Afraid. Maybe ashamed. It took me so long to see. . .to rediscover what I'd lost."

"You never lost it, you turned your back on it. Now you pop up here suddenly, expecting everything to be wonderful, the way it used to be." He turned and walked a few feet farther, then stopped again. "What about me, Kim? What about us? You just trashed our friendship as if you were emptying your life of all the clutter."

"That's not it. You have no idea what life was like for me then. How could you know? Your parents weren't killed." She hated the bitter anger that entered her tone. It was an old anger she thought she had outgrown, until this—until he attacked her without even trying to understand or show compassion. How could he still be mad after five years? "You couldn't see it then, and you can't see it now. Maybe coming here was a mistake."

His expression didn't change. "Why did you come here, Kimberly? Why now?"

"What's that supposed to mean? Why not now? I told you I'm going to work with a group of teenage girls—"

"And what else?"

Kim grimaced. "Catch up on some old friendships. But don't worry, I won't force my friendship on you." She shot him a final, angry glare, then sprinted forward along the trail until she could no longer hear the sound of his footsteps, or the sound of his voice calling her back.

two

By the time Kim reached the buildings that formed the camp-grounds, she had worked through her outburst of anger and felt bad for running away. Judging by her past performance, it would be what Adam expected of her. Maybe she hadn't changed very much after all.

Adam had changed, though. It had taken much longer than before to get him to spill his guts about what was bothering him. If their relationship still worked the old way, they'd be friends again the next time they saw each other. She hoped that wouldn't be long. She'd never forgotten how much Adam had always meant to her. And she couldn't believe he had held a grudge against her for five years. Adam didn't hold grudges. . .or at least he didn't when she knew him. Maybe she just didn't know him anymore.

She continued jogging in the direction of the stables at the far west end of the clearing. She passed the big lodge, situated directly in the center of the camp, where the ancillary staff stayed. The cabins formed a rough circle around the lodge, cafeteria, and open-air temple. East of the temple and down a graceful, grassy incline, Kings River sparkled in the early morning sunlight. That was where the campers came to crash their canoes against the rocky rapids and dunk each other in the placid, deep pool below the cafeteria windows.

"Dozer, are you here?" Kimberly called as she reached the stables. Stepping up on the paddock fence, she tentatively gave the brief, shrill whistle she had taught the horse to answer to when he was a colt. Would he still be here? If he was, would he remember?

Other horses stirred in the paddock, munching on the grain

someone had recently put in their feed troughs.

Kim was about to give up in disappointment when a huge chestnut and black Clydesdale emerged from the shadows of the stable and marched toward her with quiet grace. The feathering over his hooves rippled with each movement of his massive legs.

Tears stung Kimberly's eyes. He was still here! And he remembered her!

"Oh, Dozer, I can't believe it!" she cried as she climbed to the top of the rough wood fence. When he reached her, she threw loving arms around the big horse's neck. "You're so huge! Did you miss me as much as I missed you?"

She and Dozer—short for Bulldozer—had become close friends as soon as he arrived at camp as a colt, when Kim was just fourteen. After her parents were killed in the wreck and Kim withdrew from the rest of the world, she grew even closer to the horse, telling him her deepest fears, her deepest pain—things she didn't feel she could tell anyone else.

One night, without asking permission, she had even driven Adam's car all the way out here from Eureka Springs just to talk to Dozer. It was as if a living being as big and powerful as this horse made her feel protected and safe. But he hadn't protected her from the punishment she received when she arrived back at the Pattersons'. He hadn't protected her from her own rebellion, either, or from the consequences of that rebellion.

Several other horses in the corral ambled up to the fence and nuzzled in beside Dozer. Next to him, they looked like miniature horses. He swept his huge head from side to side in jealous warning, and they backed away quickly.

Kim chuckled. "That's right, Dozer, tell your friends to leave. Can't they see we want to be alone?"

She cast a knowledgeable eye over the horses, wondering who would be in charge of the stables this year. She'd been allowed to help out with the horses all the time when she was younger. . .back when things were normal.

Dozer nosed against her jacket pocket, nearly knocking her from her perch on the fence.

"You big fake!" she laughed. "It isn't me you love; you can smell the candy." She dug into her pocket and pulled out a round peppermint. "This what you want?"

It was. He did have a good memory.

After giving him his treat, she said a temporary good-bye and jumped to the ground. A soft carpet of pine needles covered the trail leading back to her cabin, and their scent sprang up fresh and clean as she crunched them underfoot. The sun had climbed higher, and Kim raised her face to feel its warmth on her skin. She closed her eyes against the glare.

She had anticipated this trip with alternating joy and dread for the past three weeks. If not for an unexpected twist of circumstances at work, this never would have been possible. As it was, not only was she here as a counselor, but her employer was going to be the camp doctor.

She frowned as she thought about Doss Carpenter, the young, attractive family practitioner in Branson who had employed her last year as a medical secretary. He was a good boss, easy to work for, professionally undemanding. Sometimes, unfortunately, she couldn't help wondering if his kindness toward her had something to do with his hopes for a closer relationship. She'd lost count of his invitations to dinner, a music show, a trip to Silver Dollar City—all of which she had turned down. Involvement with a man was the last thing on her mind, especially after the nightmare she was just beginning to forget.

The breakfast gong sounded down at the cafeteria, and Kim realized she was hungry, as usual. She switched directions and followed the smoky aroma of frying sausage. The steamy, scented warmth of the dining room greeted her just as she walked in.

"Kimberly Bryant!" a female voice called to her from the

line of hungry campers. A young woman with soft, blond curly hair separated herself from the others and rushed across the room toward Kim.

"Pamela Sue Reed!" Kim cried. "You did come!" The two caught each other in a happy embrace.

"I told you I'd be here in my last letter, didn't I?" Pam backed up to look at Kim. "I can't believe it's been five years since I've seen you, and you're more beautiful than ever."

"Yeah, right," Kim scoffed. "Remember what Mrs. Ames used to tell me in high school? 'Kim, if you'd just smile and keep your mouth shut, everyone would think you were pretty.'"

"She was talking about your sass, not your looks," Pam said, hugging her again. "So do you still like Branson, or are you dying to come back home to Eureka Springs where you belong?"

Kim urged her friend into line. "I don't belong there."

Pam bristled. "Of course you belong there. It's where you grew up—"

"And messed up."

"Forget that. You're back now."

"I'm just amazed the board of directors allowed me back to be a counselor. Everybody knows I left them in the lurch at the Passion play. They didn't have an understudy for my part."

"Give it a rest, Kim. I played the blind girl, and I loved it. Besides, you're not the same person you were five years ago. You were a hurting kid then, and everyone knew it."

They filled their trays and slowly, with apprehension on Kim's part, wove their way around tables to join some of the other staff members from Kim's old church. Kim glanced at Adam, who sat at the far end of one long table in deep conversation with short, baldheaded Mr. Shaw, the church youth director.

Mr. Shaw caught sight of Kim, and his serious expression

brightened. Adam looked up, too, and his eyes softened. Kim thought she detected a welcoming grin on his face, but before she could analyze it and make sure, Mr. Shaw was around the corner of the table and grabbing her in a bear hug.

"Look who's finally back, everybody! Kim's here!"

His wife, Donna, and the others at the table all joined him with hugs and kisses and a few tears. Kim could not prevent her own tears of relief and joy. She truly was being welcomed back, as if she'd come home.

"Oh, honey, you don't know how we prayed for you," Donna said with a final hug before they took their seats. "After you left and no one knew where you were, we had to learn to depend on God to take care of you."

"Donna didn't lose faith for a minute," her husband said.

Kim sat down between Adam and Pam. "Thanks, guys. You don't know. . .you can't imagine what's been going through my mind. I've been so afraid you wouldn't have anything to do with me, that you'd all given up on me—"

"Did the prodigal son's father give up on him?" Adam asked.

"No, but his brother wasn't too crazy about his return." Kim shrugged.

Adam leaned across and covered her hand with his. Though Kim still caught remnants of that quizzical expression she'd seen earlier, his smile, and his touch, were sincere.

"I'm sorry I didn't have Donna's faith," he said. "Welcome home, Kimberly."

Kim felt another smarting of tears. It felt good to be back in Adam's good graces.

The rest of them joined hands, and they bowed to give thanks for the food. Mr. Shaw did the honors, and for once she didn't mind that he was long-winded, and that the food would get cold before they could eat it. She reveled in the love she felt flowing toward her and the Spirit she felt resting within her. Why hadn't she seen this before? Why had she ever left? So much time wasted when she could have been serving God.

Adam's hand gave hers a final squeeze when the prayer ended.

She finished her sausage and eggs, and started nibbling the edges of her French toast, when a new arrival drew her attention to the cafeteria entrance.

Doss Carpenter, her employer, stood framed in the doorway, his wavy blond hair tousled by the wind, his blue eyes searching for a familiar face. When he caught sight of Kim, his tense expression eased and he waved, stepping in from the bright sunlight.

"Whoa! Who's that?" Pam whispered when Kim waved back.

"My boss. I told you about him in the letter."

Pam took another look, and her expressive hazel eyes lit with appreciation. "That's going to be our camp doctor for six weeks? He's gorgeous! Is he married?"

"Hold on, Pam," Kim warned. "Aren't you the one who's always told me that looks don't count, that it's what's inside the heart and whether that heart's right with God that matters?"

"Of course," Pam replied, not taking her eyes from Doss as he bypassed the food and headed toward them.

"Pam, he isn't a Christian," Kim said softly.

Pam blinked and turned to look at Kim. "He's not? What's he doing here, then? I thought the directors only wanted Christians to work with the children."

Kim shrugged. "Me too. That's why it surprised me when they accepted his offer at the last moment. His partners weren't thrilled, and neither was the rest of the office staff, because they knew I'd be gone for six weeks, too. Don't get me wrong; I'm glad Doss is here. He's a good doctor." She didn't mention the fact that Doss was sometimes too attentive for her comfort. "I guess I talked about this place so much at work, he decided he had to see it for himself."

Before Doss reached the table, Adam stood, walked over to the man, and greeted him.

"Dr. Carpenter?"

Doss shook his hand. "Yes, and you are. . .?"

"Adam Patterson, assisting the camp director. We appreciate your filling in for us on such short notice after our misfortune last week."

"How's that?" Doss asked, frowning.

"Our regular camp doctor had an automobile accident, and we suddenly needed someone in a hurry."

Doss stared at Adam in surprise for a moment. "I didn't realize. . .but I'm glad I could help." He glanced at Kim and winked. "My pal, Kim, was the one who convinced me to come. I fell in love with this place after she described it to me over and over and over again."

Again, the quizzical expression flitted across Adam's face when he looked at Kim. "Maybe she can tear herself away from her food long enough to show you to your office," he suggested.

"No problem; I've already found it," Doss said. He squeezed Kim's shoulder. His hand lingered a little longer than necessary before he turned toward the door. He stopped with a muffled groan as the door opened and a familiar woman walked in.

Kim barely suppressed a gasp of surprise. The woman, Priscilla Waters, was one of Doss's most regular, and persistent, patients from Branson. Priscilla had shoulder-length waving blond hair, a slender, athletic figure, and a tanned face with features that did not need makeup. She turned toward Doss with obvious determination.

Doss turned with just as much determination toward Kim. "What's she doing here?" he hissed.

Kim shrugged. "Beats me, but you're on your own, pal. I have to finish my breakfast." Grinning, she turned away from his pleading expression. She had to make excuses for him to avoid Priscilla at the office, but up here she was off duty.

"Kim," Adam said softly as he resumed his own breakfast. "Those two know each other?"

"Yes." She looked up at Adam. "Why? You know her?"

"She's our interim camp director's sister. I think she's planning to stay a few days."

"Doss will love it, I'm sure," Kim said with a sly grin.

"This may be an interesting camp," Adam said. "Since your boss is occupied, how about a ride on your Clydesdale before the kids come?"

Kim's smile widened. "Yes! All right! I thought you'd never ask."

"While we're riding, maybe we can talk about old times. Seems to me our conversation was interrupted this morning. I want to find out what you've been up to the last five years."

Kim's smile wavered. Was she ready to tell Adam everything? More important, was he prepared to hear it?

Adam watched her expression with a raised eyebrow but said nothing.

Kim forced herself to finish her breakfast, but slowly. She was stalling, and Adam surely knew it, which would make him even more curious about what she had to hide. But she wasn't really hiding anything, she was just. . .putting off the moment of shame as long as she could. She didn't even like to think about the past herself, much less share it with someone whose opinion mattered so much to her.

Wasn't that shame one of the reasons she was here? So she might help other teenagers avoid the same fate?

She might as well face up to her own.

three

Strong memories of old times flooded back to Kim as she walked alongside Adam toward the stables, the scent of cedar and pine gentle in the air, the summer sun warm. But so many things had changed. . .so much time had passed. With the help of some good friends at her church in Branson, she was beginning to forgive herself for the past and not to dwell on it. But this sudden leap backward into her old life brought taunting memories.

Adam rested his forearm on her shoulder. "Okay, what's wrong? You still mad about this morning?"

She grinned and kept walking.

He continued. "We've trekked halfway from the kitchen to the stables, and I haven't heard a word from you. If this had been the old Kim, my ears would be tired by now. Why so quiet?"

"Comes with maturity. You should try it."

"I'll think about it."

She could feel his curious glance on her, but said no more until they drew close to the paddock, and a huge shadow fell across their path.

Kim looked up to greet Dozer, but to her surprise, she found an unfamiliar, long face pointed toward them.

"Another Clydesdale!" She ran the rest of the way to the paddock fence and climbed to the top. "When did they get him? Why didn't I see him this morning? What's his name?"

Adam gave a relieved chuckle. "Thank the Lord this new 'maturity' didn't soak in too deep." He ambled up to the fence and joined Kim, stroking the horse's neck. "His name's Titan.

I christened him myself."

Kim nodded. "Sounds like something I'd have named him."

"I know."

Warm satisfaction deepened the effects of the sun on Kim's face as she stroked the rich chestnut sheen of Titan's nose. His black mane, tail, and feathering gleamed with blue-green lights. He stood a few inches taller than Dozer, though he was not as stocky.

Dozer sidled up to the three of them along the fence and nibbled at Kim's hair.

Adam reached through the fence to give the newcomer a pat before heading for the tack room.

"Titan's been with us about two years," he said over his shoulder. "Bryson was probably riding him this morning when you were here."

Kim jumped from the fence to join Adam. "Bryson? Who's he?"

"He's one of the permanent fixtures here at the camp now. He takes care of the stables and. . .security."

Kim took the bridle Adam held out for her. "Security? Here? Why would—"

"Why would we need security here at the camp?" Adam picked up two soft saddles—Clydesdale-sized—and another bridle. "Things are changing out here; you know that. We're having more and more problems with marijuana growers in the area, and it has been suggested there's an illicit drug lab somewhere in the national forest area. We brought Bryson in when we decided to bring troubled teenagers to the camp."

Kim followed Adam into the paddock. "He's here to help control the kids?"

"To protect them." His dark brown hair fell over his forehead, and he tossed it back with his hand. "No noncampers allowed on-site except parents and relatives on visiting day."

"How does it work, mixing troubled, non-Christian teenagers with Christian kids in the same group?"

"We'll see. The Christian kids are here specifically to display the love of Christ in practical, everyday living. They're part of a mission action group. They're really dedicated kids to stay up here for six weeks."

Kim helped Adam saddle and bridle the horses, then allowed him to help her onto Dozer.

"Whew! I'd forgotten how far up it was on this guy." She took a deep breath. "I think the air's thinner up here."

Adam mounted Titan and led the way toward one of Kim's favorite trails.

"You remembered!" she called as she caught up with him.

"I had no choice. You always insisted on riding this trail. Besides, the leaves are thicker on the trail here, in case you fall. Been a while since you've ridden?" he asked when he saw her slipping her hand through the saddle loop. "You never had to hold on before."

"It's been five years."

Adam glanced sideways at her and shook his head. "What happened to you? I could never keep you away from the horses before."

Kim shrugged. "As you said, things change."

"In what way? What—"

"Adam, tell me about the other counselors in the camp this year. Don't they have some kind of training? I'm surprised I was chosen to counsel a group of girls without anyone to guide me."

"We have our ways of screening prospective counselors."

"I don't remember being screened."

"You filled out an application, didn't you?"

"Well, yes, but—"

"We have someone on staff here who spends several months every year checking out applications, making calls, and asking for references."

"You mean someone actually gave me a good reference?"

"Sure did. Someone at your church—several people, in fact. I read the report. Good report, Kim. I thought surely you must have turned on the charm at your new church."

Kim turned and glared at him and caught him grinning at her. "At least I have charm to turn on, unlike—"

"So when do we talk, Kim?"

She hesitated. "I thought we were talking."

"Small talk. I know where you've been for the past two years, active in your church in Branson, taking basic college courses and working for Doss Carpenter, staying out of trouble. . . You implied this morning that we might catch up on everything that's happened since you left Eureka Springs. Three years are a mystery to me, and to Mom and Dad."

"They're a mystery to everyone in my life now, Adam," Kim said softly. She grew physically braver and urged Dozer to a faster pace. "Remember those verses you kept quoting to me after my parents died? Wasn't it Paul who told the Philippians, 'Forgetting what is behind and straining toward what is ahead, press on toward the goal'?"

"Yes, and he was right, but—"

"And didn't you always tell me that no sin was too black that it couldn't be cleansed by the blood of Jesus Christ?"

"Of course, but—"

"I've remembered those words, Adam. When I had nothing else to hold onto, I remembered. The truth of what you told me all those years ago was what gave me the courage to return here and face my irresponsible actions. But maybe I'm not strong enough yet to face all of them."

The trail narrowed, and Kim rode ahead of Adam for several hundred yards. When there was room again, he rode up beside her.

"Kim, I'm sorry. I really blew it this morning."

She glanced sideways to see his tanned face tinged with self-recrimination, his dark green eyes unseeing, his brow creased in deep thought for a moment. He looked across and held her gaze.

"I shocked myself this morning," he said. "I didn't realize, until I discovered who it was kicking me and fighting me so desperately down there on that dark trail, that I would react that way when I saw you again." A bemused smile hovered at his mouth. "Believe me, I thought about it a lot since discovering you would be here this year. By the way, I haven't told Mom and Dad. Not yet. I guess I wanted to see for myself what kind of person you had become before—"

"Before you took the chance of seeing your folks hurt again."

He looked away.

"I understand," she said, even though it stung. "Are you still reserving judgment?"

"I called them after breakfast and told them you were here. They were all for driving down immediately, but I told them to give you a little time. Maybe on visitor's day they can come. That'll give us two weeks, and we won't be breaking any camp rules."

"Easing them in gradually?"

"Easing all of us in gradually."

They reached a familiar sun-dappled clearing, and he reined in. "Let's rest here for a few moments. If you haven't ridden in five years, you'd better take it gradually, too."

Kim had always been drawn to this quiet cove in the woods, where a modest outcropping of rock was now decorated by a growth of maidenhair fern and Queen Anne's lace.

She found a spot in the sun and made room for Adam to sit beside her after he tethered the horses.

"I think you were in the middle of an apology," she reminded him when he joined her.

He grinned, and for a moment the brilliance of his green eyes rivaled the sunbeams filtering through the oak leaves above them. The grin faded as he grew serious again.

"Your sudden departure five years ago threw all of us into shock, not only Mom, Dad, and me, but your church family. Mom and Dad felt as if they had failed you somehow—"

"But they didn't. They did everything possible—"

Adam raised a hand. "I'm just telling you about our reactions. They were desperate for word from you; they prayed for you constantly. But for a long time, I couldn't bring myself to pray for you. That was wrong, of course, I know. But I was so angry with you, so bitter. . ." He shrugged. "It took me several months to recover." He plucked a grass blade and absently spun it between his fingers. "I felt betrayed. I guess I depended more on our companionship than I'd even realized."

"When did you stop being angry?" Kim asked.

"I thought I recovered during my third year at college in Bolivar. I had to prepare a sermon on forgiveness. As I studied for that sermon, I realized that I didn't know enough about forgiveness to write two paragraphs, much less a sermon. I spoke about it to one of my professors, and he prayed with me about it. Then I started to pray for you. It's kind of hard to pray for someone and stay mad at them."

"I know."

"But when I saw your name on that application, some of my anger returned. I had to resist the temptation to call you immediately."

"What would you have said?"

"Who knows? You saw my reaction this morning."

"I understand your anger," Kim said softly. "I was angry at myself, as well. You'll never know how sorry I was about everything, and now I'm sorry I didn't get back in touch with you and John and Kate, at least to let you know I was okay."

"Why didn't you?"

"Because for a long time, I wasn't okay. I think, subconsciously, I wanted you to find me and rescue me, but pride kept me from calling for help. After a while, I convinced myself that you had not bothered to look for me at all—"

"But we did. Of course we did!" Adam took her hands and held them. "Don't you know we would have come if we knew where you were? What did happen, Kim? Why did you need rescuing?"

Kim saw the earnestness in his face and felt the warm strength of his hands, and her eyes stung with tears. "I asked for what I got, Adam. And I'm okay now, so it doesn't really matter what happened then." She gently drew from his grasp and stood. "Come on, riding that monster is easier on my nerves than this little conversation."

"I think you're wrong, Kim," Adam said as he helped her back onto Dozer and handed her the reins. "I don't think you're okay now, or you wouldn't be having so much trouble facing the past."

She adjusted her seating and sat looking down at him from her lofty height. "I'm facing it."

"No, I don't think you are."

"How would you know?"

"Why don't you feel comfortable talking to me about it? Why can't you just tell me what happened?"

"Why do you have to know everything?" She scowled at him. "Okay, here's part of it: I lived on the streets of Kansas City, ate my food out of trash barrels, and resorted to frequenting a Salvation Army shelter for the homeless. I got arrested for sleeping in an unlocked car and arrested again for stealing food—that wasn't for me; it was for an old man I'd discovered on the streets. I refused to tell them I had identification, and they turned me over to this nice lady at the Salvation Army shelter. It isn't on my record because they never knew who I was. Are you satisfied, Adam?"

The expression of pain on his face cut her deeply.

A sudden need for more honesty spurred her a little further. "After all that, I was too ashamed to invite you to my wedding. Okay, Dozer, we've worked out the kinks," she said. "Let's see if you can still run."

four

"Ouch! I forgot I was riding a skyscraper," Kim cried as oak leaves slapped her in the face. She struggled to stay on the galloping horse, more memory returning in ever more painful ways: You didn't race a Clydesdale beneath low-hanging branches. Horse mane flicked her arms, and fear kept her gripping the saddle for several hundred feet, unable to slow Dozer to a walk.

Only when she heard the other monster galloping up behind her did she find the courage to release her clutch with one hand and pull back on the reins.

Titan drew abreast.

Adam took the reins from her and stopped both horses. A red scratch on his cheek told Kim a similar oak branch had caught him. "Kimberly Bryant, you almost got yourself knocked off that horse. Are you crazy?"

"Yes; some things don't change."

"That's not what I mean—"

"I was crazy to say anything about the marriage. I wasn't ready to talk about—"

"Then don't."

She blinked at him and tried to read the expression in his eyes.

"If you're not ready to talk about it, don't. I may not be ready to hear about it." He still held her reins. He looked at her for a long, uncomfortable moment, then glanced down at the reins in his hands. "I didn't think you could shock me. All kinds of thoughts went through my mind after you left, horrible thoughts. It occurred to me several times that you might be wandering the streets of some city, homeless, or even worse. I even thought of drugs, or that someone might have picked you up and forced—"

"Yes, I know, drugs, prostitution, the underbelly of life. You thought I'd turned my back on everything my parents and your parents ever taught me." She heard the frustration in her own voice; he'd been ready to believe anything of her. And yet, wasn't he right? Almost.

"You were a kid, barely seventeen. You were a total innocent and certainly not capable of taking care of yourself on your own."

"It's nice to hear you had regard for my resourcefulness."

"I never dreamed you'd get married."

"Neither did I. And I never thought I'd be a widow a few months later."

"A widow?"

Kim nodded. "The guy I married was not the guy I thought I married. Until then, I never realized what a dupe I was. . .how naive. I'd been so sheltered; I expected everyone to treat me the way they always had back home. . .like a kid." She sighed and gazed out through the forest. In spite of its own battle between good and evil, Eureka Springs was a paradise compared to the rest of the world.

She glanced at Adam and grimaced at the shocked expression he continued to try to disguise. "I think that's enough for today's session," she said. "Any more may kill you. Here, let me get that leaf out of your hair. Come on; we've got kids to meet."

❧

The sound of running water and the sight of steam seeping out from beneath the closed bathroom door told Kim she was late. Some newcomer was already taking advantage of one of the two showers. But she didn't have a chance to investigate.

"Hi. Who's hoggin' the shower already?" a youthful, strident voice demanded from behind her.

Kim turned and was instantly charmed by a mischievous

expression in the pixie face staring back at her. At least eight inches shorter than Kim, the girl had scruffy, short black hair, and eyes almost as black.

"Hi yourself," Kim said. "I don't know who's 'hoggin' the shower,' but there's another if you need one."

"Nope, just curious." The girl stared at Kim with disconcerting boldness.

"I'm Kimberly Bryant, your counselor for the next six weeks."

The girl's jaw dropped in disbelief. "Counselor! I thought you were one of us campers." She narrowed her eyes. "You don't look old enough to be a counselor."

"Twenty-two going on fifty, honey." Kim felt a return of her doubts about this job. She'd studied the files and knew the background of each girl, but what did those files miss?

"You don't look twenty-two," the girl said.

"You must be Carrie."

The girl's eyes widened. "Right!" she exclaimed. "How'd you know?"

"I'm good." So this was the fifteen-year-old who had been caught and held for the possession of cocaine, and who had run away from home last year. An irrepressible charmer.

Carrie's black hair framed an oval face with a flawless complexion. Although her dark eyes were smudged with too much bright makeup, the girl's features held a promise of beauty that took Kim's breath away. This tiny package of mischief would keep things exciting. As if Kim needed more excitement.

"So who's in the shower using up all the hot water?" Carrie whined.

The water faucets squeaked as the water went off. Kim shot Carrie a look of reproach.

The girl spread her hands. "It worked, didn't it?"

The bathroom door eased open, and the wet girl who stood there wrapped in a towel, brown hair dripping with water, glanced from Carrie to Kim.

"I–I'm sorry; I didn't know I was doing anything wrong." She pulled the towel tighter around her shoulders, her soft brown eyes wide and nervous.

"You weren't," Kim assured her. "Carrie was just teasing."

"Yeah, teasin'," Carrie agreed, "but since you're out, why get back in?"

Kim nudged Carrie with a warning elbow as she opened the cupboard along the wall for another towel. "Here, use this to dry your hair. You must be Gail."

The girl gave a start. "How did you know?"

Carrie leaned forward conspiratorially. "She knows everything about us: our grades in school, our height and weight—she says she's our counselor, but I think she's a cop or a social worker." She winked at Gail, who responded with a hesitant smile.

Kim felt a rush of compassion for Gail. Being an unwed mother would be hard enough, but to give that baby up for adoption must have been especially difficult for this timid sixteen-year-old. Her file said she was suffering from depression. Kim would have to keep a close watch on her. With prayer and patience, maybe the atmosphere of the camp would do its work, as long as Carrie didn't bully her.

"Hello, anybody here?" came a singsong alto voice from the cabin doorway. In stepped a beautiful young girl with long auburn hair. She wore a bright turquoise silk dress and carried an expensive-looking leather suitcase. Another girl entered behind her, a younger version of the first, who wore a silk dress in pink that complemented the slightly lighter shade of auburn in her hair.

"Let me see. . .you're Michelle and Joni?" Kim guessed. When the girls nodded, she grinned. "Do you think they placed you in my cabin for a reason?" she asked, gazing pointedly at their red hair.

"Don't tell me I have to be seen with this group!" Carrie

joked. She sobered under Michelle's cold stare.

"Well, girls," Kim announced, "pick your beds. The community closet is across the room over there, and we each have a chest of drawers."

For the next thirty minutes the girls eyed each other with hesitant curiosity as they silently unpacked their cases and put their clothes away in the chests and the closet. Carrie's tattered case flew open to reveal an overabundance of equally tattered jeans and T-shirts. Gail's modest case held only a few pieces of clothing. Both girls watched with undisguised envy as Michelle and Joni put their dresses and slacks on hangers and slipped them into the closet.

The final two campers for Kim's cabin arrived just as Michelle placed her last pair of pants in the closet.

The new arrivals, Natalie and Susan, were sisters who came from a church in Springfield. Kim watched them as they immediately introduced themselves to the other girls and jump-started the chatter that had been noticeably lacking until their arrival. Natalie, the brown-haired older sister, was pretty but overweight, and barely taller than Carrie. Susan, the only blond in the group, was slender, with friendly blue eyes and freckles.

Kim breathed a silent prayer of thanks for these newcomers, for their friendliness and lack of self-consciousness. She couldn't help comparing the backgrounds of the girls. Natalie and Susan came from a closely knit Christian family, whereas Michelle and Joni had been bounced back and forth between divorced parents for the past year. Carrie's father had left when she was a baby, forcing her mother to struggle to support the two of them. Gail had both parents, but had made a serious mistake and was paying for it now.

Kim hoped she was mature enough to handle any crises that would arise in the next six weeks.

"Okay, girls, they're breaking us in right," Kim said, raising her voice above the chatter until the campers fell silent.

"We're having a worship service in the temple in a few minutes and—"

"Already?" Carrie exclaimed. "No way. I'm tired."

"You weren't too tired to scare Gail out of the shower a little while ago, so I think you'll live," Kim told her. "Besides, we go straight from the service to the cafeteria. After that we'll make an early night of it if you're really tired, even though we are having a s'mores party afterward, bonfire and all."

"But do we really gotta go to the service?"

"That's what she said, isn't it?" Michelle snapped, shooting Carrie a scornful glance.

"I'm not asking you, I'm asking—"

"You heard me, Carrie," Kim said. "Get changed."

"Changed?" Gail said from her bed in the corner. "What are we supposed to wear?"

"Dress the way you would for church."

"Ha!" Carrie said. "How's that? I don't go to church."

"B—but I don't have clothes for church," Gail said. A flush crept up her neck.

"No problem," Michelle declared. "I've brought all kinds of things. You can have a sundress." She reached into the closet and pulled out a pretty green dress.

Gail stared at her. "You mean it? You'd let me wear this?"

"Sure, I don't need them all, anyway." Michelle shrugged. "They're just payoffs from my father for getting lost for six weeks."

"Shelly!" her sister exclaimed.

"Shut up, it's true!"

"So? Everybody in camp doesn't have to know about it!"

"They'll know soon enough anyway."

Kim cleared her throat. "Time to start getting dressed. Come on, let's get a move on."

Carrie dragged her gaze from Michelle and turned to Kim. "What did you interrupt for?" she muttered. "The good stuff was just starting."

In spite of Carrie's continued grumbling, Kim managed to coax them all into their clothes and out the door toward the temple before the huge brass bell rang in the bell tower.

She felt a glow of expectation as she and the girls sat down near the back. She found Adam sitting behind the podium and was surprised to see him watching her. When he caught her eye, he winked at her. She grinned and waved, then glanced beside her to see Carrie observing with intense interest.

"You know him?" the girl asked, her black eyes wide with admiration.

Kim nodded. "He's an old friend."

"What a beaut."

Kim bit her lip, suppressing another grin.

Doss Carpenter walked in, and Kim saw Michelle nudge her sister, Joni. Both heads followed his progress across the auditorium.

"Maybe camp won't be so bad, after all," Michelle whispered to Joni.

Carrie turned to see who Michelle was talking about. She suddenly stiffened beside Kim.

Kim nudged her. "He's too old for you," she teased.

Carrie nodded soberly and looked away.

Kim watched the girl, puzzled. This wasn't the behavior of a girl enthralled by a good-looking guy. Carrie seemed surprised. . .no, unsettled. But when Susan whispered something to Carrie, and she responded normally, Kim put the incident out of her mind.

Kim couldn't prevent a surge of pride when Adam spoke to the congregation of campers. She'd heard him preach before, of course; he had spoken at their old church in Eureka Springs on youth Sundays even before he graduated from high school. But years of school had polished his words until the truth shone, and those same years of experience gave him more depth from which to share his own special, clear viewpoint of the Scripture they read.

Kim glanced across at her girls where they sat listening with rapt attention. She hoped they were actually listening to his words and not just enjoying his masculine attraction. If only those words would reach them and they would gain some understanding of the message. How could she convince them of all the beauty life held for them when they trusted in God and not in drugs, money, or casual sex?

Too soon, the organist played the first notes of the benediction. The rest of the campers skittered out of the temple in a race to the cafeteria, but Kim and her group lagged behind. No one seemed eager to leave when they spotted Adam weaving his way around kids toward them.

"May I join you for dinner?" he asked when he reached them. He'd promised Kim earlier that he would, when she admitted how nervous she was about this camp.

"We'd love it," Carrie replied, edging in closer to him.

As they walked across the grass, Kim listened to the whispers and muted giggles between the girls. Nothing had changed. Adam had always been well liked, even when his complexion wasn't as clear and his manner wasn't as relaxed and easygoing. His attraction lay not so much in his good looks or personality as much as in his intensity for Jesus Christ. Kim had always been able to clearly see the light of God's love shining through Adam.

In the cafeteria, Kim watched her campers as they selected their food. Michelle shook her long, dark red hair behind her shoulders and took modest portions of fried chicken, potato salad, and bread. She made sure her younger sister, Joni, did the same. Natalie and Susan took more generous portions as they called out to other campers they remembered from past years. Carrie piled her plate high with food, but when she looked at Gail's nearly empty plate, she put some of her own in it.

"You gotta eat something," Kim heard her mutter as they left the line to find a table.

Kim smiled to herself.

"You're doing it already," Adam remarked behind her. "I knew you would."

"Doing what?"

"You're studying them. I can hear that brain of yours clicking already, deciding how to help each girl." He placed an extra piece of chicken in her plate. "Here, you'll need extra energy to keep up with this bunch for six weeks."

Kim felt a flush of satisfaction warm her face. "Thanks, but if anyone reached the campers tonight, it was you. I've never heard you speak so beautifully before."

Carrie darted back through the crowd toward them. "Hey, you guys, we found our table."

"Lead the way," Adam said. "And later," he told Kim softly, "I'm ready to hear more about your adventures in KC."

five

To Kim's disappointment, Adam excused himself from the group as soon as they finished dinner. The girls pleaded with him to stay, but allowed Kim to herd them out of the cafeteria toward the bonfire that blazed down by the river. Bright flames licked the sky and reflected from the water, illuminating some nearby volleyball players with a golden glow.

After the girls left to watch the coed game in progress, Kim found her way over to the Shaws and relived old memories as she held marshmallows over the fire. Pam joined them a few moments later.

"Hey, girl, we've got some catching up to do." Pam rummaged through a grocery bag and handed Kim more marshmallows. She then brought out some chocolate bars and graham crackers. "We've got to do this right, even though I know my jeans won't fit me by the time I leave here."

"They will if you intend to keep up with me," Kim warned.

"I doubt it," Pam complained, her gaze resting on Kim's slender figure. "How do you still eat like a horse and keep your weight down?" She gestured to her own comfortably plump waistline.

Kim swallowed a bite of marshmallow. "Exercise."

"I'd have to exercise all day every day for months to lose this."

"I did."

"What? How?"

"I hiked the Appalachian Trail."

Pam gaped at her. "You're kidding."

"No."

"When?"

"I started four years ago. It took me two years to complete, with breaks in between for winter, of course, and to work to support myself."

"You hiked the whole thing?"

Kim nodded, grinning. "From Georgia to Maine."

"You really did that?"

"I did. I went alone, carried my own tent and everything."

"How did you afford it?"

"I saved up from my old job, bought and dried my own food, then had some friends from Springfield mail new supplies to me by general delivery every week to specified places I expected to be."

"Was it hard?"

"It was one of the hardest things I ever did, and I'll always be glad I did it. I'll have to tell you more about it sometime. It's a great way to lose weight, if you're dedicated enough." She paused, then added softly. "It's a great way to come to grips with God. I think it's what I needed to make enough peace with my past so I could allow God to control my future. I was so mad at Him for a while. . . ." She shrugged. "I'll tell you about that sometime, too."

Pam watched her for a moment. "I'd like that, Kim. Really. Meanwhile, I'd like to follow you around for a few days. I'm gaining weight just watching you eat."

Kim stood up and brushed off her slacks. "You can start by coming with me to find some more sticks. We've run out, and I see more kids coming down from the cafeteria." She marched toward the woods.

A few moments later, Pam exclaimed, "Whew! You built some muscles on that hike. I have to run just to keep up with you." She selected a branch, contemplated it, then discarded it. "Where did Adam get off to? I thought he was eating with you."

"He was. I guess he got full."

Pam selected another branch and stripped the leaves from it.

"I know you think of Adam as a brother. I mean, you two were always so close, and you were part of the family and all. . ."

Kim glanced at her friend quizzically. "Yeah?"

"Well, I don't think Adam sees you as just a sister. At least not anymore. Maybe he never really did. I always wondered. When you left, it really hurt him."

"I know that now." Kim quickly doused a little flame of hope that flared.

"I heard he dated a few times in college, but I don't think it was anything serious."

"I'm not surprised. Adam always said he wanted to finish college and seminary before he even thought about marriage."

"Well, he's been out for a while now. Maybe that's not the only reason he never got serious with anyone else."

"Meaning what?"

Pam shrugged and leaned against the trunk of a tree.

"No, no, keep moving," Kim said. "Exercise, remember? And don't get any ideas about Adam and me. Nothing's changed."

"That's exactly what I'm getting at." Pam straightened from the tree and giggled. "Do you remember the night you went out with Greg Heller?"

"You mean Heller the Hustler?" Kim grimaced. "Why didn't anyone tell me his nickname until after that night?"

"I guess we figured you knew. Everyone else did. It's a good thing Adam found out about it and went to find you."

Kim shrugged and considered a few branches. "It wasn't so bad. I had everything under control when Adam arrived. When Greg got too pushy, I just sent him into the store to get me a candy bar, and I locked all the doors when he was gone."

Pam gasped. "You never told me!"

"I promised I wouldn't tell anyone, because I left him standing out in the rain. Adam didn't find me until I used Greg's car phone to call home." Kim laughed softly. "It was one of the highlights of my junior year, so you can imagine what the rest of the year was like."

"What would you have done if Adam hadn't come? You didn't know how to drive, remember?"

"I would have called Adam's uncle, Clem Elliot, since Adam's parents weren't home. But Adam remedied the problem the next day. He taught me how to drive his old junker."

"His prized possession," Pam mused. She leaned against a fallen log and slanted a glance at Kim. "Did you ever think that, possibly, Adam surpassed the duties of a big brother?"

Kim shook her head. "Never considered it for a moment." She paused. That was a lie. "Well, almost never. Did I ever tell you about the time I took a drink of kerosene? I was ten and Adam was a very mature twelve. Our parents had all gone out together that night, and left him home to keep an eye on me."

"What happened?"

"He called 911, then called our parents at the restaurant where they were eating. The ambulance got there before our folks did, so Adam insisted on riding with me to the hospital. When our parents reached the emergency department, my dad gave permission for them to pump my stomach. In all the excitement, they forgot about Adam, and he stayed there with me while they worked on me." She shook her head and chuckled. "He was green by the time they finished. How can a guy feel romantic toward a girl when he's been through all that?"

Pam shook her head. "If romance is all sweetness and light that falls apart when the beauty fades, then romance has nothing to do with love."

"You're talking about the wrong kind of love."

"I don't think so. I've watched him around you today. I don't think he ever got over you."

Kim forced a laugh. "Come on; you need some more marshmallows. Your imagination is working overtime."

Pam watched her friend in the reflection of the bonfire glow. "I don't think you ever got over him, either."

A shadow separated itself from the woods and came toward

them. "Hey, what's goin' on?" Carrie called out. "Kim? I thought maybe you'd left us already."

"Left you?"

"You know, bailed out. Six weeks is a long time to get stuck with someone like Michelle."

"I heard that," came Michelle's deep, well-modulated voice that made her sound older than sixteen. She stepped over to join Kim and Pam. "I bet you're the one who bails out, Carrie. You can't stay straight for six weeks."

"No betting in a Christian camp," Kim said absently as she watched another, taller figure come toward them.

"Hey, there's Adam," Carrie called. "Knew he couldn't stay away."

"Me too," Pam said softly so that only Kim could hear.

"That's right." Kim stepped forward to meet Adam. "You never could resist s'mores, could you?" she asked him.

"Nope," he said. "And how many have you had so far? Ten, fifteen?" He smiled at her through the darkness. Perhaps it was a trick of shadow from the fire, but the smile didn't seem to reach his eyes.

"I lost count after five. Can't be too much more, though, because I've been out here hunting for sticks so you latecomers can have your share."

"I appreciate it." He held up a jar of peanut butter. "Extra crunchy, just the way you always liked it."

Kim caught her breath. "You remembered! Just for that I'll make you a batch of my own special recipe. Would anybody else like to taste—" She turned to find the girls following Pam to the other side of the bonfire, where a new group from the boys' side of the camp had just arrived at the volleyball court. "Looks like we get to eat the jar all by ourselves."

"Suit yourself, but I prefer the peanut butter inside the jar, myself. You've acquired some weird tastes since you left." Adam settled on a log nearby and gestured for Kim to join him. He pulled a plastic spoon from his pocket. "This is to spread the peanut butter. How's it going with the girls so far? You seem to be building a good rapport with them."

Kimberly grimaced. "It's early. I'm still nervous."

"You shouldn't be. You've always had a way with people. You'll do fine. You work with people every day, don't you?"

"Sure, but I'm not responsible for them. Doss is."

Adam stretched out more comfortably and stuck some marshmallows on one of the branches Kim had collected. "Do you enjoy working for him?"

"Sure. I mean, it's not going to be my career, but it's helping me get through school at SMSU."

"Your parents left money for that. Why didn't you claim it?"

Kim shrugged and pulled some graham crackers out of a box. She took the spoon from Adam, spread peanut butter on top of the graham crackers, then sprinkled chocolate chips on top of that. "I'm not sure why, Adam. I guess I felt I owed that money to John and Kate. I mean, they supported me for a year."

"They didn't expect pay, and they never touched the money. It's yours, plus interest. It will always be yours. You don't have to work and go to school at the same time. You could have been out by now if—"

"I know, but I'm not, okay?" she snapped.

Adam glanced at her sharply.

She sighed and shook her head. "Sorry. I just don't deal with what-ifs. It's not logical."

"I'm the one being logical here. This is not a what-if. The money is there, and it's yours. Use it, and stop being so independent."

Kim could not suppress a sudden grin. "You haven't changed; you're just as bossy and impatient as ever."

"And you are as stubborn as ever." He held up the marshmallows. "Just right; nice and tan and melting, not like those charred ruins you ca'' roasted. Tell me about your job," he said as he carefully placed the marshmallows on top of the prepared crackers. "You obviously like your employer, or you wouldn't have recommended him for this position."

Kim glanced at Adam in surprise. "I didn't recommend him. I was surprised to hear he got the position. He's not a Christian."

"Do you know Priscilla Waters?"

Kim smashed a graham cracker on top of her concoction and handed it to Adam. "Trying to get me fired? You know I can't tell you about patients."

"So she's a patient of Dr. Carpenter's?"

"Adam! I didn't say that."

He smiled, and once again his smile did not reach his eyes. "No, you did not."

"Why do you want to know? Why all this sudden interest in my employer?"

Adam took a large bite of the s'more and spent the next moment chewing.

"Adam?"

"Maybe I'm jealous."

"Very funny. What's the real reas—"

"I think you were going to tell me more about marriage." He swallowed and looked at her.

"I didn't tell you that."

"You implied that you would tell me when I was ready to hear more. I'm ready."

"Maybe I'm not ready to remember it."

"I thought you said you had learned to forgive yourself and go on with your life."

Kim shook her head and shrugged. "Fine, I got married two days after I turned eighteen. I met the guy at the mission in KC, decided in just a few weeks I was in love with him, and married him. I fell for his lines about 'forever,' then found out afterward he was a druggie, not only a user but a pusher."

Adam grew very still. "Drugs? Did you—"

"Get high? Not willingly."

"What does that mean?"

Kim took a deep breath and let it out slowly. "It means there were a couple of times I had something slipped into my food or soda. I didn't realize it at the time, and I still don't have any memory of those times. Someone who was there told me about it later."

Adam stared at her in outraged shock. "Your husband drugged you?"

"Come on, Adam, this isn't a particularly pleasant subject for me. I don't want to think about it anymore, okay? It's humiliating. I remember some strange people who came over and slept on the living room floor. I remember waking up to find the whole apartment littered with drug trash and liquor bottles. That was when I contacted the police. They raided the place, and my. . .husband escaped. He was later shot and killed robbing a pharmacy. Do you have to know every single detail?"

He took a deep breath and stared into the bonfire for a moment. "No, I don't have to know anything; I just feel as if I need to hear it. I want to understand what you went through, and what you did. I. . .want to come to terms with it."

"What if you can't?"

"I will."

"But how do you—"

"Adam," came a deep bass voice from the shadows. A man stepped into the light of the bonfire. Kimberly had caught a glimpse of him earlier in the cafeteria. He was at least a couple of inches taller than Adam at six-feet even, and he had the shoulders of a linebacker. His dark hair and eyes reflected the glow of the flames, but his expression held no warmth.

Adam took a moment to answer, as if mentally shifting gears. "Hi, Bryson. What's up? Oh, excuse me, Kimberly, this is Matt Bryson. He watches things at the camp, takes care of the horses." His voice sounded friendly, but forced. "Bryson, have some dessert. It's Kimberly's specialty, and it is the best s'more you've ever tasted."

"No thanks." The new arrival's deep, gravelly voice grated.

"Matt, I like the new Clydesdale," Kimberly said. "He's gorgeous."

"Oh? You've seen him already?"

"Yes, Adam and I went riding this morning."

"Both the Clydesdales are good horses. Titan doesn't have Dozer's heart, or his intelligence. Adam, I need to meet with you. We're having some. . .difficulties, and I would like your input."

Adam had picked up another graham cracker. "Sure. Name the time."

"Now. Sorry." Bryson nodded toward Kim. "I'm afraid it's urgent."

Adam put the graham cracker in his mouth, chewed and swallowed, and stood to leave. "Sorry, Kim. See you later." He hesitated, turned back. "By the way, don't go running around the camp in the early morning hours by yourself. You could break a leg, and we wouldn't know where you went."

"Fine, go with me. I'll be leaving around five-thirty from my cabin. Bring a flashlight if you're worried about it."

"Five-thirty!"

"I want to be back before the girls wake up. Take the offer or leave it."

He scowled at her. She shrugged.

"Fine, I'll be there," he said. "Just wait for me, okay?"

"I'll wait ten minutes. Nice to meet you—" The two men had already disappeared into the darkness.

Kim shrugged and leaned back against the trunk of a tree. She could see Carrie and Michelle on the volleyball court, and the rest sitting on the sidelines cheering them on. That was encouraging. Maybe Carrie and Michelle would get along after all.

With the girls occupied, Kim decided to gather some more sticks. That proved to be more challenging than before because the light from the bonfire had died down to glowing coals. She bent and straightened in the shadows several times, selecting and discarding. She wandered farther from the fire and had just decided to return when voices reached her from a few yards away.

"Priscilla, be reasonable. I told you I wanted out months ago. I don't want to keep going on like this." The voice belonged to Doss Carpenter, Kim's boss. He did not sound happy.

Kim froze in surprise. His involvement with women had become a legend around the office, especially women who didn't like to let go, but as far as she knew, Priscilla Waters had never been one of those women. No one ever thought he would become involved with a patient.

"Sorry you feel that way." Priscilla's voice was clipped with anger, and the coldness in it made Kim shiver. "I had hoped I wouldn't have to remind you how much you owe me already. You're not out of this by a long shot, mister."

"Look, Priss, I'll make it worth your while, I promise. I can pay—"

"You'll make it worth my while, all right," she snapped. "Or do you want me to tell your partners what's been going on?"

There was a long silence.

"No," Doss said after a long pause. "Don't say anything to them. I'll stay in."

"Of course you will," Priscilla said. Her voice remained cold. "Now walk me back to my cabin. I've had enough campfire fun for one night."

The two strolled away. Kim stood staring after them in the nighttime chill. She tried to remind herself that Doss and his love life were none of her business, but she couldn't help wondering. What on earth was going on?

six

In spite of the late hour that Kim and the girls had retired the night before, Kim awoke early the next morning to the sound of groaning outside the cabin. For one crazy moment, she thought about the occasional reports of bears migrating to these woods from farther south, but the groan turned into the hum of an airplane—a low-flying airplane. It came so close, it sounded as if it might land right at the camp.

Kim glanced at the lighted dials of her watch, hoping the airplane hadn't awakened any of the girls. It was five-fifteen. Time to get dressed and meet Adam outside. Would he show up?

Yes, she knew he would. Adam always did what he said he would do.

No one else stirred. Kim put on her clothes and brushed her teeth, keeping the bathroom door closed. She didn't want to wake the girls, but she for sure didn't want to kill Adam with morning breath.

The hinges of the front door squeaked, but no one called to her as she stepped out into the predawn chill.

"You're late."

The voice came from the nearby darkness. Kim nearly cried out in alarm.

"Adam?" she whispered. "That you?"

He stepped into the glow of the camp light, his broad shoulders large and reassuring. "Who else would be crazy enough to come jogging with you out here in the middle of the night?"

"Shh! The girls are still sleeping. Come on." She took a few steps away from the cabin toward the lodgepole pine forest to the west of the camp. "It isn't the middle of the night; it's after

47

five-thirty." She braced her right leg against the fallen trunk of a tree and bent to stretch.

"It's inhumane. Why do you torture yourself like this?"

She touched her toes and grinned. "Don't be such a grouch. It was your idea to come with me. Why aren't you stretching? Do you want to pull a muscle?"

"I want to go back to bed." He pulled out a flashlight and switched it on. "Follow me. At least I'll be sure you won't get hurt this way."

"That's not the way I'd planned to go."

He ignored her and kept walking.

"You bullheaded, macho. . . ," Kim muttered softly, then smiled again. Adam had never been a morning person, but he would soon learn that a few things had changed.

She turned in the opposite direction and followed a narrow path that skirted the edge of the forest and circled the camp.

"Kim, are you coming, or are you going to just stretch your muscles all day?" He called from the other trail.

There was silence while she kept walking.

"Kim?"

"Would you please keep your voice down?" she called softly. "Do you want to wake the whole camp?"

The sound of shuffling footsteps reached her as Adam retraced his own trail at a jog. "Where are you? What are you doing?"

Kim chuckled to herself. "I'm going the way I had intended to go before you invited yourself along. You can come with me or you can go back to bed. Just leave me the flashlight."

He caught up with her and matched his pace to hers as she eased into a gentle jog. The beam from his flashlight attracted strange shadows that leaped and danced at the motion of his body. They circled the camp in silence, then Adam stopped at the head of the trail he had first attempted.

"Now will you go with me this way? At least compromise?"

"What's so important about this trail?"

"I helped construct it. You've never been on this one, and I thought you might like it."

"Why didn't you say that earlier?"

"I was sleeping. Okay, Kim?"

"Of course. Lead the way, oh, mighty bearer of the light."

She hated it when he did that: explained his actions so that she felt guilty for her reactions. But she didn't hate it enough that she didn't enjoy running behind him, watching the flex of his muscles, listening to the rhythm of his breathing. They ran up a long incline, and as they reached the top, dawn broke over the brooding, tree-enshrouded hills. The birds greeted them with the first songs of the day. Low mists drifted around the trunks of the pines, hiding the grass and foliage beneath.

Kim ran silently, peering through the trees with a growing joy as she caught glimpses of the golden horizon. But she forgot to watch her steps and Adam.

Her toe kicked a pine cone and sent it hurtling toward Adam's feet. Stepping aside, she veered into a bush and tripped on its overhanging foliage. Adam stepped on the cone and slipped, teetering backward as Kim slammed into him from behind.

They landed in a heap of arms and legs on the needle-strewn trail.

"Ouch!" Kim cried as Adam's leg landed on her arm.

"Sorry!" Adam rolled aside. "You okay? What happened?"

Kim took time to catch her breath and make sure there wasn't any serious damage. She shook her arm. Not bad. She wouldn't have to pay Doss a visit.

"I'm okay," she said. "How about you?"

He stood up, then reached down to help her. "Just a little damaged pride. I forgot all about Hurricane Kimberly. Remember? You used to pull stunts like this all the—"

"Yeah, yeah, I know." She took his hand and let him pull her up. "It must have something to do with you. I haven't done anything like that in a long time."

He didn't release her hand, but continued to look down at her. He grinned, then sobered, tenderly touching her right arm.

"Are you sure you're okay?"

"It was my left arm you fell on."

"Oh." He released her right arm and took her left. "Think it'll need x-rays?" He touched it and probed with his fingertips. "Any pain? Bruising?"

"Time will tell, but I don't think it's hurt that badly."

He reached up and pushed some strands of long golden hair from her face. "How about the rest of you?" He put his hands on her shoulders. "You took quite a tumble. Think we knocked anything out of place?"

She stood staring at the strong planes of his face in the morning shadows. "I'm. . .fine."

"You sure?" He smiled again. "You're sounding winded."

She took a deep breath and exhaled, then stepped backward. "Of course I'm winded; we just ran up a mountain. I notice your breathing isn't that great either."

He released his grip on her shoulders and put an arm around her, easing her back along the trail. "Technically, there are no mountains in Missouri, not in the true sense of the word—"

"I was speaking figuratively."

"Of course you were." He stopped and retrieved the flashlight from the side of the trail where it had flown during their accident. "I think we'll bring another one along in the morning."

"You mean you're planning to do this again tomorrow?"

"For the next six weeks, whenever you jog in the dark, I jog in the dark."

"But Adam, I've jogged in the dark for years. I've been on my own—"

"I know, but bear with me, okay? Old habits are hard to break. I'm not sure I want to break this one, watching after you, playing big brother, seeing to it that you don't get into more trouble—"

"More trouble? What do you mean more trouble? I can take care of—"

"Ever meet a bear on that Appalachian Trail?"

Kim stopped and stared at him in the growing light. "Pam told you about the hike?"

"Actually, it's on the follow-up report we have in your file. Someone from your church mentioned it, and the interviewer thought it was so interesting she decided to add it. I found it fascinating, and it scared me to death."

"Why? I'm alive, aren't I?"

He slowed his steps, his dark, thick brows drawn together in concern. "It scares me that you still have that old impulsive nature that landed you on the streets of Kansas City, eating out of trash cans."

"Oh great. I knew I shouldn't have told you about that. I knew it. When are you going to stop playing big brother and start being my friend?"

"I've always been your friend."

"No, you've always been my own personal policeman. You always felt as if you had to keep me in line, keep me from getting into trouble." She glanced up at him and felt a rush of compunction for the look of hurt that crossed his face. "I'm sorry, Adam," she said more gently. "But I'm a big girl now. I may still be impulsive, and I may still fall down and skin my knees from time to time, but you've got to learn to let me take the knocks myself. You can't take them for me, or I'm not going to grow."

They walked for several moments in silence, watching the woods get lighter, watching the mood of the day change from one of bright expectancy to one of a promise fulfilled. They reached the edge of the camp, within sight of Kim's cabin, when Adam stopped.

"Is that why you left?" he asked, his voice quiet and reflective.

"Was it because of me?"

"Oh no. No, Adam, it wasn't because of you. It was because of me. I couldn't bring myself to forgive God for the accident that took Mom and Dad. You know that. You did know that, didn't you?" She watched his face, reached up to touch his cheek. It was rough and unshaven. "Adam, didn't you?"

"Are you sure?" he asked at last.

"I'm positive. Tell me you haven't blamed yourself all these years."

He didn't answer, but his expression did. He turned to stare out into the forest.

"Adam, please don't do this to me." She grasped his shoulder and urged him to turn back toward her. "I never meant to hurt you like that. I wasn't even thinking about how you would feel; I was only being selfish, thinking of my own pain."

He turned back. "And I wasn't thinking of yours. I should have been. I wouldn't leave you alone and give you time to heal. How could I have been so blind, Kim? You'd lost your parents, and I wanted you to behave as if nothing had happened. I didn't even give you the chance to grieve."

"No, Adam, don't do this. It wasn't your fault."

"Wasn't it?" He stood looking down at her, and the morning light caught the depth of his green eyes. "Partly?"

She shook her head, but she couldn't answer. They looked at each other for a long moment, until the temple bells rang the wake-up call, and broke the connection.

He took a deep breath and looked away. "Kim, I have to ask you to do something for me during camp. Please don't leave the grounds without me."

"What?" She felt a flash of irritation. After all they'd just talked about, he was going to continue playing the bodyguard?

"Don't wander off alone. This is not the Appalachian Trail, and I told you there have been some reports of marijuana growing in the area. These growers take their harvest yield seriously, and they aren't afraid to take measures to protect their crops. If you want to go hiking, just call me, will you?"

She frowned at him. "Sure. Whatever you say."

"Kim, I'm sorry." He hesitated. "I'm really not trying to play policeman, not this time, not now. I am sharing some responsibility for the camp, though, and for your safety."

"It's okay, Adam."

"Hey!" A young, penetrating voice called from the open front door of the cabin. Carrie stood there in her nightshirt, black hair spiky and tousled around a face refreshingly devoid of makeup. "What's goin' on? You get lost in the woods?"

"You'd better take care of your little flock," Adam told Kim. He waved at Carrie and turned to jog along the trail toward his own place at the lodge.

She watched him for several seconds before turning to join Carrie.

Pam was right; nothing had changed with Adam. He still wanted to play the role of protector. Maybe Pam was right about other things, too, but Kim didn't want to think about that right now. She didn't dare.

After all this time, she still had to battle a longing to be more to him than just a friend of the family. Her teenaged crush had never died, and she was no longer a teenager. It would be so easy to imagine that Adam's tenderness and concern betrayed more than friendship or a brotherly devotion, but she'd been through that pain before. It wouldn't happen again.

seven

All day Monday, Kim couldn't stop thinking about her morning run with Adam. Perhaps because of those thoughts, the day went smoothly as she and the girls went to morning praise, breakfast, and the rap session afterward.

The girls weren't as hard to manage as Kim had expected. In spite of their differences, and perhaps because of the calming influences of Natalie and Susan, the seven of them got along well together a large part of the time. Even some of the rivalry between Carrie and Michelle became more friendly than spiteful—not all of it, but some. The schedule of activities was so varied and interesting that the girls were forced to cooperate with each other. Even though that cooperation was begrudging at times, it encouraged Kim.

After a short initial awkwardness, Carrie became a particular favorite with the rest of the kids at the camp, her earthy humor and street smarts providing a novel attraction for some of the other girls. Kim only hoped the irrepressible teenager didn't impress the others in the wrong direction.

Even Gail came out of her sad shell on occasion, especially that afternoon when Kim took a group out to explore the hiking trails. The sport appealed to Gail. The heavy sadness in her pinched face lifted more and more often as she listened to Kim compare the Christian walk with God to a hike in the forest.

"Notice that we're all walking together to share the experience," Kim told her fellow hikers. "We encourage each other. If one of us stumbles, a buddy will help us find our footing again. If one of us sees something beautiful in the woods or in the sky, we share it with the others. A church works like that.

54

If one of us makes a mistake and forgets to walk with God, others gently help and remind us until we regain our footing. If one of us is hurting, others will pray with us. If one of us has received a special blessing from God in her life, she will call the others in her church family to praise God with her. When you become a part of God's family, you are truly a part of a new family here on earth. You won't be alone."

"But what about our own families?" Gail asked. "We won't have to leave them or anything like that, will we?"

"Your earthly family will always be your earthly family," Natalie said. "Susan will always be my sister, and our parents will always be our parents. But they are also part of my church family, because they know Christ."

"But what if my family doesn't know Christ?" Gail asked.

"Then you introduce Him to them," Susan said. "But do you know Christ?"

Gail shook her head.

"Do you want to know Him?" Natalie asked eagerly.

Gail looked down. "Isn't that what this camp is for? So we can learn about Jesus?"

"That's right," Kim said. "Just listen and learn."

That evening, at the praise service before dinner, Kim convinced the girls to sit closer to the front of the auditorium. Pam and her campers sat with them. To Kim's surprise, Doss Carpenter came in and found a seat beside Pam.

"What's *he* doing here?" Carrie muttered to Kim.

Kim raised a brow at her. "He's our camp doctor. You know that. You saw him last night."

Carrie continued to glare at Doss. "I thought he had a girlfriend. What's he doin' with Pam?"

Kim shrugged, wondering the same thing. She glanced around, searching for Priscilla Waters, but the woman hadn't been to any of the Bible studies or worship sessions.

Adam didn't join the girls at dinner, and Kim wasn't the only one who was disappointed.

"Even a preacher has to eat," Carrie grumbled as she cut her smothered steak with the side of her fork. "Why can't he eat with us?"

"What's the matter?" Michelle taunted. "Can't you even eat a meal without a guy to tease?"

Carrie snorted. "You got no room to talk. I saw you watching that counselor across the aisle at the praise session tonight."

"Don't get carried away, you two," Kim warned. "We have plenty of time to meet people and form friendships. Slow down."

She took a bite of fried okra and glanced up to see Doss weaving his way around the tables toward them. He looked up, his gaze centered on Carrie. Suddenly he turned and joined Pam's group at the other end of the dining area.

Kim glanced over at Carrie, who was busy arguing with Michelle and hadn't noticed the incident.

"I don't guess Adam's hungry tonight, huh?" Carrie remarked a few moments later. "He still hasn't come in, and I've been savin' this chair for him."

"Give it up, Carrie," Michelle said. "He's not coming or he'd be here by now. Besides, it's Kim he's interested in, not you."

"I know that."

"Uh, girls, it's not—"

"Excuse me, may I join you?"

Everyone at the table turned around to find a plump, gray-haired lady standing beside the empty spot at the table with a food tray in her hands.

"Of course," Kim said. "Have a seat. I'm Kimberly Bryant."

"And I'm Mrs. Morgan." The lady put down a tray of cookies and milk and pulled out the chair beside Carrie. "It's been a few days since I've had a chance to chat with anyone; they keep me so busy back there." She leaned toward Kim. "I'm strictly volunteer, but I don't know what they'd do without me. I worked at a camp down south of here earlier this spring, and I had my hands full." She pushed the tray of cookies out to the center of the table. "Anyone want one? They're my specialties, molasses and peanut."

"Thank you, Mrs. Morgan. They look—"

"Yes," the lady continued, "those cooks at the last camp hated each other. Two of them disagreed on how many eggs to put in the pancakes, how much flour to put in the bread, and how much bacon to fry for breakfast. It turned out that the cooking wasn't the problem at all. One cook's son was going steady with the other cook's daughter, and the two kids decided to run away and get married. Well, one lady blamed the other, and the fight was on."

"I'm sorry to hear—" Kim began.

"It wasn't a great place to work, anyway, so I just started coming up here. They need volunteers in the kitchen every evening, and I putter around the rest of the day in a little garden I've started. . . ."

Mrs. Morgan talked nonstop for the next fifteen minutes. The rest of the girls finished their meals and stared at the lady, glassy eyed.

Carrie leaned over and nudged Kim, sighed, rearranged her dishes, then yawned loudly.

"Do you like herbal tea, Kim?" Mrs. Morgan asked.

Kim jerked to attention. "What? Herbal tea? Yes. . .I suppose I—"

"Good. I'm mixing up a batch, and it should be ready in a couple of weeks. You'll be the first to taste it," she declared, rising from her chair. With a quick nod of her head, she walked away.

Kim stared after her.

"Hurry!" Carrie exclaimed. "Let's get outa here before she comes back."

Kim and the girls scrambled to their feet, emptied their trays, and dashed out the door. When the last girl came out, Joni leaned with a sigh of relief against the door.

"Whew! Where did she come from?" Michelle demanded.

Kim burst into laughter. "You should have seen your faces." She sobered quickly. "She's probably very lonely."

"That's right," Susan said. "We should have compassion for her and make an effort to be friends with her while we're here."

"Why?" Carrie challenged.

Susan glanced at Kim, then Natalie. "Because a Christian should show the love of God to everyone, not just to the people who are fun to be with."

"What, exactly, is a Christian?" Carrie challenged.

Kim led them toward their cabin. "A Christian is someone who knows she has sinned and turns away from it, accepting Christ's death as payment for her sins."

"What's sin?" Carrie asked. "I've heard the word today, but I don't know what it is. Sounds like a foreign language to me."

"Sin is when you mess up, big-time," Natalie said. "You know, like you do something bad that you should go to jail for, but someone else goes for you."

"Or someone dies for you," Susan added.

"We all mess up," Kim said. "We do things that take us away from God. So God sent His Son, Jesus Christ, to pay for what we've done."

"Oh yeah?" Carrie said. "What about you, Kim? You've never done anything wrong. You probably always go to church and help lonely old ladies, and cook dinners for people."

They reached their cabin, and Kim opened the door to let the others through. "Everyone does wrong, Carrie. We all mess up. I've done more than my share."

"Oh sure. Like what?" Carrie demanded.

Kim hesitated. What good would it do to tell these girls about her own life?

"She probably skipped school once, or something like that," Joni said.

"Yeah or talked back to a teacher," Carrie jeered. "Big deal."

"I did skip school," Kim said. "In fact, I left school before I graduated, and I had to get my GED later."

"Wow!" Michelle said. "I wish my parents would let me leave school early."

"My parents were dead," Kim said softly.

Shock silenced the room.

"I decided I was big enough to make it on my own, so I left my hometown behind and went to the big city," Kim continued.

"Which one?" Natalie asked.

"Kansas City."

"What happened?"

"I got lost." Kim felt a catch in her throat. "I was lost for a long time."

Natalie took a couple of steps closer to her and hugged her arm. "How'd you find your way back?"

"A nice lady reminded me of Christ's love for me." Kim smiled and brightened. "Who's up for a board game? I brought six."

Later, as Kim lay waiting for sleep, she shifted impatiently and punched her pillow. She hadn't come here with the intention of reliving her past; she'd come to help others. Why had it all gotten so personal? Everyone she used to know asked her where she'd been, especially Adam. She'd expected that, but not this sharing with teenage strangers.

Closing her eyes again, Kim tried to sleep.

A low rumble reached her ears, and her eyes flew open. This was getting ridiculous. Was that an airplane again? It sounded close enough, and low enough, to land, but there had never been an airport anywhere near Sunrise Retreat. What was going on out there?

She sat up and listened until the rumble disappeared. It had not landed, but had flown away as before.

♨

The following days, Kim and the girls lapsed into an enjoyable routine—routine, that is, for anyone living with six energetic, mischievous teenage girls. She enjoyed the morning jogging sessions she spent with Adam, and was encouraged when the two of them began praying together about the camp and about her girls individually. She felt the need for prayer because she knew she wasn't reaching the most troubled girls on the levels where they were hurting the worst. In spite of her revelation, they didn't seem to identify with her. She was one of the *Christians,* with whom they had nothing in common.

The girls proved eager to explore every activity the camp offered. Gail went with Kim on all the afternoon hiking trips, for which Kim had been chosen guide since she knew these forested hills and trails so well. Others, like Carrie, preferred to stay by the river and swim during the warm afternoons. All of them had reached that precarious stage when nothing was as much fun as meeting the boys. Kim found herself pushed into the role of chaperone.

Carrie, Kim realized early, was an outrageous flirt. She craved attention, especially from the male species, and her impulsive nature often led her into mischief she couldn't handle. Kim found, to her chagrin, that she had to watch Carrie for signs of danger. Once, the girl locked herself in the marina dressing room and couldn't get back out.

Three days after the marina incident, as Kim casually sauntered back toward her cabin from a visit with Dozer, she heard agitated cries coming from the river. She stopped, listened, then shook her head. It had to be the boys, since it was their turn in the swimming area.

But a piercing scream shattered Kim's calm. That was definitely feminine, and definitely Carrie!

eight

Kim turned and raced toward the riverbank. What was that kid up to now? She wasn't even supposed to be near there when the boys were swimming.

At the sight of Carrie, Kim gasped in horror. The swimming area was downstream from a length of forbidden rapids. Carrie was directly in the middle of those rapids, desperately clutching an outcropping of rock. A canoe, wildly careening away from her, told its own story. No one below had seen her yet and must not have heard her above the sound of the rapid water.

The terrified girl saw her. "Kim! I can't swim! Help—" She lost her grip and plunged beneath a cascade of water.

Kim raced to the edge of the riverbank and kept going, shoes and all, to protect her feet from rocks. The current caught her when it reached her waist, tossing her like a feather in the wind. She kept going, and it threw her against a boulder, striking her in the side and knocking the breath from her lungs, but she forged deeper with a practiced stroke until she reached the spot where Carrie had gone under.

After searching above the white water for a bobbing black head, Kim dove beneath the surface and reached out blindly in all directions. Nothing. She surfaced, fighting the water, then gasped a lungful of air and plunged down again. She reached out, and her hand caught at something soft. Carrie!

With a frantic heave, Kim thrust the girl's limp body up toward the life-giving air, then came up beside her, struggling for breath. The current had swept them past the rapids toward a tranquil pool, but Kim was weakening quickly.

"Help!" Kimberly spluttered. "Someone help us!" Then she

sank, unable to keep both herself and Carrie above water.

Her open, gasping mouth took in its first gulp of water, and she coughed, feeling blackness attack her. Her feet touched bottom, and she pushed herself to the surface for more air. As she did so, strong hands gripped her waist and lifted her up. She choked and wheezed, still holding Carrie with the little strength she had left. Her rescuer towed them both toward the bank.

"It's okay, Kim, I've got you," came Adam's deep voice beside her.

Other voices reached her from the shallows, and as soon as they could, the boys took Carrie's body from Kim.

Both were laid on the grass nearby, and Kim lay gasping for breath as Adam worked over Carrie.

It seemed as if long moments passed before Kim heard Carrie draw her first, fighting breath. Adam had turned her onto her stomach, and she coughed up water. Nearly weeping with relief, Kim struggled to pull herself up, only to collapse when her weakened limbs would not hold her.

Adam reached over and drew her into his arms. He squeezed her so tightly for a moment that she pushed against him. Still, he did not release her entirely, but kept his hands on her shoulders.

She looked up at him in concern. "Are you okay?"

He stared at her for a moment, then shook his head. "No, Kim, you scared me." His voice held accusation. "You can't guess at the thoughts that shot through my mind."

"Sorry, but what was I supposed to do, let Carrie drown?" Kim pulled from his grasp.

They both turned to see the girl, awake now, breathing well, and surrounded by several of the boys and counselors. Someone had called the doctor, and Doss and the camp nurse came rushing toward them.

"Of course you did the right thing," Adam said at last. "You couldn't have done anything else. It's just that. . ." He hesitated.

"Just that what?" Kim demanded. "I shouldn't let myself get into situations like this?"

He frowned. "Don't get so upset, I was just worried, that's all." He reached forward and touched her shoulder again.

"Well, stop worrying, okay? I'm a big girl, remember? I've taken care of myself for a long time." She forced a smile to try to hide some of her irritation, but she knew he saw through it. He had always said her bullheadedness would get her killed someday, but today it was Carrie's bullheadedness that had nearly done it, and Kim wasn't willing to take the blame for it.

She stood unsteadily to her feet, brushed some of the grass from her drenched clothes, and stepped over to see about Carrie, who seemed physically fine now. When Kim turned back around, Adam was gone.

She grimaced in self-reproach. He was just worried about her. Why did she have to get so defensive?

She checked once more on Carrie, then went to find Adam. He had probably gone to his room at the lodge.

A few minutes later, after changing into some dry clothes, she stepped up to his door and raised her hand to knock, when she heard a deep, angry voice from inside.

"If that kid can't be controlled, we'll have to send her home. And if that counselor—"

"You're talking about Kimberly," came Adam's voice. "She'll be okay. And we can't send Carrie home just because she acts up a little bit. This camp is for kids just like her. What did you expect?"

Kim stood frozen beside the door. She knew she should leave—these doors offered far too little privacy—but they were talking about *her*. She recognized the man's voice; it was Matt Bryson, the man who had come to get Adam at the bonfire the other night.

"Besides," Adam continued, "Carrie will get suspicious if we send her home, and if she suspects something, she might ask questions. We don't need that kind of attention."

Bryson grunted. "What about Kim? She goes running around camp in the dark every morning. This could be dangerous for us."

"I know," Adam said. "I'd rather send her home and keep her out of this, but trust me, that isn't going to happen. I know her. I've been going with her in the morning, and I'm keeping her away from the drop site. That's the only place that's vulnerable. I think that's the best we can hope for right now."

There was a long silence, then the sound of footsteps. "Have it your way," Bryson said. "I'll talk to you about this more later, but keep an eye on those girls." His steps came toward the door.

Kimberly scrambled back toward the lodge entrance. All she needed was to be caught eavesdropping on them.

Frustration knotted her stomach as she stepped out of the lodge into the late afternoon sunshine. Worse than the frustration were the disappointment and pain. She had led herself to believe Adam went jogging with her, and sought out her company and prayed with her, because he wanted to renew their old relationship. But something else was going on. He didn't want to spend time with her; he just didn't want her running around the camp in the early morning alone.

Why not?

Her thoughts went back to that first morning, when she had run into Adam on the trail. And the car.

Did he know something about that? If so, why all the subterfuge?

She reached the stables in time to see Dozer coming out into the paddock, and only then did she feel the tears that had coursed down her unheeding cheeks. She felt like an idiot. She felt used. And by Adam, of all people.

"I thought you'd gone riding once already today," came Adam's voice from behind her.

She sniffed and swiped at the tears on her face with the back of her hand. "I haven't and I'm not." She didn't turn around.

There was a long silence. "Kim? Are you crying?"

She didn't answer.

He stepped up beside her, ignoring Dozer's attention-seeking snort. "Your nose is red. It's a sure sign you've been crying."

She stepped up and smoothed her hand along Dozer's long, silky forehead.

"You're blaming yourself, aren't you?" Adam asked gently, coming up beside her again.

Kim frowned and glanced at him. "What do you mean?"

"I'm talking about Carrie. You can't blame yourself for the actions of another confused teenager."

Relieved by the change of subject, Kim raised a brow at him. "Sounds familiar."

"Why?"

"Haven't you been blaming yourself for my actions five years ago?"

"No. I've been blaming myself for my own actions. It's different. Look at how I behaved with you today, for instance." He sighed and reached up to scratch Dozer's ears. "I'm sorry, Kimberly."

"Oh, really?" She sniffed, dabbed at her tears with the back of her hand, and forced a smile. "Sorry you saved my life today?"

"Sorry I snapped at you." He turned and looked at her, a slight smile touching his eyes. "I did pull you out of there, didn't I?"

Once again, Kim thought about the conversation she had just heard and remembered that Adam didn't want her here.

"Congratulations. You're a hero." She sighed and turned away. "I've got to see a doctor about a patient."

"Can't I go with you?"

She kept walking as she shook her head. "I don't want Carrie to think we're ganging up on her."

He caught up with her in spite of her protest. "I'll walk you there."

Kim stopped and glared up at him. "Would you back off? You're not my shadow, and you don't have to keep an eye on me in broad daylight." She winced at his hurt and bewildered expression.

"Kimberly Bryant, what's gotten into you? Why are you talking like this?"

She refused to lie, but she wasn't about to tell him that she'd stooped to eavesdropping through closed doors. "Isn't that why you go running with me in the mornings, so you can keep an eye on me and keep me out of trouble?" She cut him off before he could answer. "I'm sorry, Adam, but you're just going to have to trust me a little more. Don't carry the hero bit too far."

This time when she walked away, he didn't follow.

❧

Kim walked through the infirmary door into air-conditioned chaos. Doss knelt in the center of the small waiting area, with files piled up all around him. He glanced up at Kim and frowned.

"If you're looking for your misbehaving camper, she isn't here."

Kim stepper farther into the room. "You released her already?"

He picked up a file, opened it, then closed it and put it in another stack. "I didn't have a chance. She refused to see me. She went back to the cabin." He gestured at the files. "Do you know what these are? Medical histories on every single kid in camp. Nobody bothered to organize them; they just left them for me to do. They think I'm a secretary." He raised a brow at her. "I don't suppose you'd—"

Kim raised a hand. "Not me, I've got kids to corral." She shot him a teasing grin. "I know someone who'd probably love to spend time helping you."

"Who's that?"

"Who else? Priscilla Waters."

A cold mask filtered down over his face. "Forget it," he

snapped. "I'll do it myself. These files are confidential, and I don't want just anybody pawing through them."

Kim blinked at him. "Sorry I mentioned it. Maybe I can find some time in the next few days to help."

"Good. I'd appreciate it. I can trust you to keep your mouth shut." He smiled at her, a forced smile that looked more like a grimace. "You should find Carrie at your cabin. I think Pam was going to wait for you there."

Kim stepped into the cabin a few moments later to find Pam sitting in a chair reading and Carrie lying on her bed in the corner, her back turned to the room.

Pam got up and motioned to Kim. "She cried herself to sleep," she whispered. "She won't talk to me. Maybe she'll talk to you. I've got to go check on my own group."

Kim thanked her, then walked over and sat down beside Carrie on the bed. For a few moments she let the girl sleep, trying to ignore her grumpy inner voice, which said that if Carrie had slept last night, instead of dreaming up new ways to get into mischief, she wouldn't be so sleepy now. Kim had to remind herself what it felt like to be an unhappy teenager. Carrie might act tough and self-sufficient, but it was all bluff. There was an emptiness inside her, and she was trying to fill it with the wrong things.

But how could she be taught to reach for the right things? She needed the love of God.

"Carrie? Honey, would you wake up?" Kim bent over the girl and brushed the short black strands of hair away from her cheek.

Carrie came awake with a sudden jerk, as if from a bad dream, groaning with a protest as her eyes flew open in terror. She saw Kim, and flung her arms around her with a sob.

Kim held her gently. "It's okay now. You're safe."

"I'm sorry," the girl croaked, as a flood of tears burst forth, quickly soaking the shoulder of Kim's blouse. "I didn't think that would happen."

Kim continued to hold her, rocking her as she would a small, frightened child. "It's over now."

"But we almost drowned. Both of us! I didn't mean to do that to you."

"What about you? We didn't want you to drown, either."

Carrie hiccuped and sniffed. "It doesn't matter about me," she whispered.

Kim drew back and held Carrie's shoulders, forcing the girl to look at her. "Of course you matter! Why do you think I jumped into the river to get you?" Kim reached over for a tissue from the box on the chest of drawers, then used it to blot the tears from Carrie's face. "You matter very much."

Carrie shook her head. All the makeup she usually wore had been washed away by river and tears, and she looked so young and defenseless, Kimberly wanted to cry.

"I'm just a stupid troublemaker. I'm always causing problems. My mom has to work two jobs to support both of us, and if I weren't around, she'd probably be married again and wouldn't have to work so hard."

Kim wondered if Carrie's mother had told her that.

"Are they going to send me home?" Carrie asked.

"No. You might get to have a talk with one of the other counselors, but I don't think they're going to send you home. Now, why don't you tell me about this afternoon? What were you doing with that canoe?"

Carrie blew her nose and shifted uneasily on her bed. "It was stupid, really."

Kim nodded. "Taking a canoe into the rapids when you can't swim is a dumb thing to do; never mind that it was also off limits. What I want to know is why." She patted Carrie's shoulder. "Why did you do it?"

Carrie sighed. "I didn't think it would be that hard. I mean, you showed us how to paddle and everything Monday."

"I also told you never to go out without a life jacket, and we were in the calm water on Monday, not rapids. You still haven't told me why you did it."

Carrie hunched her shoulders. "I didn't see why we couldn't swim with the boys, and I thought that would be a good way to protest. I thought it would be fun to paddle right into the middle of the boys during their swim time." She grimaced. "It mighta worked, too, if that stupid rock hadn't caught me."

"That rock never moved. It had a right to be there, and you didn't. You broke the rules."

"But I came to camp to have fun. What fun is swimming without boys?"

Kim bit her lip to suppress a smile. "Believe me, you can have fun without boys. You don't have to be with them all the time. Was it a boy who helped you drag the canoe all the way to the head of the rapids?"

Carrie lowered her gaze and shook her head.

Kim raised a disbelieving eyebrow. "It wasn't? You couldn't have done it yourself; the canoes are too heavy. Who helped you?"

Carrie squirmed. "I can't tell."

"Yes, you can."

The girl shook her head adamantly. "I'm in enough trouble. I don't want to turn my friends against me, too."

Kim sighed. "Did you bully Gail into helping you?"

Carrie narrowed her eyes at Kim, and Kim automatically knew the answer.

"You can make that poor girl do anything you want her to, Carrie. Don't force her into anything like that again."

Carrie held Kim's gaze, and for a moment, Kim thought she was going to rebel.

"Camp should be a fun place for everyone, Carrie, not just you. Gail deserves to have a good time, and she doesn't need someone she cares about urging her into mischief."

Carrie's eyes widened. "She doesn't care about me."

"Why else would she be so willing to do what you ask?"

"You just told me that I bullied her."

"Not physically. Come on, Carrie, you know what I mean. She likes you. Be her friend. She needs a friend."

Carrie held her gaze for a moment more, then lowered her eyes. "Okay."

"And please promise me you won't do anything else like you did today."

Carrie frowned and said nothing, and Kim knew there would be more excitement in the coming weeks with this girl. Wasn't there a way that Carrie's bravery and strong will could be directed into better pursuits?

"I shouldn't have gone into the rapids," Carrie said at last. "I understand that rule now. But why don't we get to swim with the boys?" She shook her head. "I still don't understand that."

Kim smiled. "You don't have to understand every rule before you follow it. The directors who made the rules understand the temptations teenagers can have toward members of the opposite sex. They want to keep you pure."

"But we swim together at home," Carrie muttered.

"The directors don't have any control over your environment at home, but they do here." Kim grinned and gave Carrie's shoulders a final squeeze. "Don't feel bad, though. I used to complain about the same rule. I've been finding out that there are usually good reasons for the rules we have, and even though we may not understand them all the time, it's our job to follow them."

Carrie set her mouth stubbornly. "I'm almost an adult. People should have to tell me why I have to follow the rules."

Kim sighed. "That's where faith comes in—faith in someone besides yourself. Here at camp, we have to have faith in the counselors and directors, just like Christians must have faith in Christ."

Carrie looked at Kim and frowned. "How can you have faith in what you can't see?" She lowered her voice. "Besides, I don't want to trust the adults in this camp. They're not trustworthy."

Kim raised a brow. "Who isn't?"

Carrie looked away nervously.

"You don't like our camp doctor, do you?" Kim asked.

"Nope."

"Why not?"

No answer.

"Did you know him before you came here?"

Carrie set her mouth in a straight line and refused to answer any more questions.

That night, as Kim lay listening to the peaceful breathing of the girls in the other beds, she struggled to go to sleep. This camp was not turning out at all the way she had hoped, but it was turning out the way she had feared. She had feared she might have a situation like the one with Carrie, and she didn't know how to handle it. What was she supposed to say to the girl? She'd rebelled, herself. She could identify also with Michelle and Joni's feelings of abandonment. She'd felt abandoned by her own parents. She understood Gail's depression. The only two kids in her group she couldn't identify with were Natalie and Susan—the two healthy sisters.

With a sense of frustration, Kim slid out from under her blanket and crept over to the window to look out at the moonlight. Maybe she was a bad influence on these girls. Without baring her soul, and her past, to these near strangers, how was she going to reach them?

nine

Kimberly jogged in silence beside Adam the next morning as the sun rose in a clear, milk-blue sky. She could sense his confusion at her silence, but she could think of nothing to say. Gone was the warm camaraderie they had rediscovered after all the years apart. He'd asked her a few questions about the incident with Carrie yesterday, and at her noncommittal answers, he had fallen into step behind her on the trail. The course went faster than usual, but it certainly wasn't as much fun.

"Kim, wait," he said as they neared the end of the final trail. He caught up with her and took her arm. "Are you okay?"

She took a moment to catch her breath, looking anywhere but at Adam. "I feel fine."

His worried green eyes finally caught hers and held them. "Are you sure? Something's not right. Did you hurt yourself or something yesterday when you pulled Carrie out? You're not acting right."

She forced a smile. "How am I supposed to be acting?"

"You know, like your usual, chatterbox self. Ever since yesterday you haven't even acted like you wanted to talk to me."

"Maybe I haven't wanted to talk much to anyone." It was true. The girls had noticed her silence as well. It wasn't all because of Adam's conversation with Bryson yesterday, although that was part of it. Too many things were happening that bothered her.

"I told you yesterday what the problem was," he said.

She raised a brow at him. "Oh? What's that?"

"You're taking too much responsibility for what Carrie did

72

at the river. You've always done that. You blame yourself for anything that goes wrong."

She shook her head and turned toward the cabin. "That's ridiculous."

"Is it? I bet you've been telling yourself that you're a horrible example for your girls, and that you shouldn't have come here. Camp isn't what you expected."

Surprised, she looked up at him and tripped on a rock.

He caught her arm and grinned. "Told you so."

She grimaced and gently pulled away. "Nothing is ever what we expect. I'll talk to you later, Adam."

"Wait a minute; what about our prayer?"

"Later," she said over her shoulder. She was sulking, she knew. The course she had taken at church on building healthy relationships had taught her that she needed to talk about things that upset her, not bottle them up. But she told herself she wasn't bottling them up; she was treading warily, judging by what she had overheard yesterday. Adam didn't want her here. She was an imposition. How could she enjoy prayer with him when his words from yesterday kept coming back to her?

As soon as the girls went to their morning craft class, Kim wandered toward the stables. Maybe Dozer could cheer her up the way he had done in the past. A welcoming nicker greeted her as she climbed the corral fence, and Dozer rushed forward, nearly knocking her from the top rail in his exuberance.

"Hey, watch it, you bully!" she chided with a smile. "I was just here yesterday, you know." She wrapped her arms around his handsome neck and pressed her cheek against his with a sigh. "It's nice to feel wanted. I wish I felt the same way with the rest of camp. What am I doing wrong, boy? Carrie still picks fights with Michelle and nearly got herself killed yesterday. It won't get any better with me as counselor. Adam thinks he has to play nursemaid. That Bryson guy wants to kick Carrie out of camp. Doesn't he even realize what this camp is all about?"

The horse stood still, as if considering her words seriously, until Titan came stomping up and pushed his way forward.

Kim rubbed the other horse's nose for a moment, until Dozer's snorting, head-tossing jealousy forced her to push Titan away in order to keep from being knocked from the fence. She laughed and hugged Dozer, then jumped down and went to the tack room for saddle and bridle. If Dozer was in this good a mood, maybe he would stand by the fence long enough for her to get on, and she wouldn't have to call someone to help her mount.

To her surprise, she was allowed to slide onto his back with ease; he didn't play his usual trick of stepping away from the rider just as she attempted to slide onto his back.

"Good boy, Dozer!" She patted his gleaming neck and urged him away from the corral fence. She heard a snort and turned to see Titan shaking his head accusingly at them. "Sorry, boy, maybe next time."

It felt exhilarating to set out by herself with Dozer after all these years. The old rebellion in her urged her to ride away the whole morning, exploring land around the camp, maybe even swimming Dozer across Kings River to check out trails she used to know. The responsible side of her told her she wasn't supposed to wander off the property. Besides, she had campers depending on her now.

Dozer instinctively headed toward her favorite trail, one they had often traveled together. It felt good to allow something bigger and stronger than herself take the lead. She trusted Dozer. As the healing balm of silence and solitude began to settle over her, she realized that some of her old bad habits had taken control of her life again. Instead of transferring her pain and worries from her own weak shoulders onto those of Jesus Christ, she'd been harboring them, carrying them herself, even while she complained to God about the pain.

"Dear Lord," she whispered, as Dozer carried her deeper into the woods, "please forgive me, once again, for my lack of faith in You. Please conquer my unbelief, and let me depend on Your strength, not my own. Just use me, Lord, and make me more capable of being used."

She knew she was here at this camp for a reason, but she didn't know what God's reason was. She also knew that one quick, simple prayer was not going to change the controlling habits of a lifetime, but she knew once again to let go. Maybe this time it would be longer before she tried to wrest the reins of her life from God again.

Just the act of prayer lifted her up. She wasn't alone; God was always with her. She took a deep breath of the fragrant air, still cool from the morning. A single meadowlark warbled its song from a nearby fence, and Kim relaxed.

Dozer slowed and stopped at the edge of a miniature field, thickly covered with wildflowers. He nuzzled the ground, and sauntered toward a stand of lush, green grass. Kim slid to the soft, damp ground and removed his bridle so he could wander at will through the field and munch. She knew she could trust him not to wander too far, not with the smell of peppermint candy in her pocket.

She strolled over to an outcropping boulder nestled in amongst the trees, and sat down to watch the Clydesdale graze.

To her delight, two deer ventured out to join him, unaware, for the moment, of her presence. They cavorted around the field like two merry schoolchildren at recess, apparently playing a game of deer tag.

Their grace and swiftness amazed Kim, and she sat in silence, not willing to alarm them by her presence. They ran across the field unaware of her and oblivious to Dozer to the point that one of them almost dove between the horse's back legs. It jumped lightly to the side when Dozer snorted and jerked his huge head around in alarm.

Kim shook with silent laughter at Dozer's expression, and at first she didn't see when both deer leaped toward her. She glanced up in time to duck as a quick leap sent them soaring high over her head and into the thicket behind her. She gasped and whipped around. What had startled them so suddenly that they hadn't been aware of her?

Dozer raised his head and pricked his ears toward the trail. Kim glanced that way, then grimaced. Doss Carpenter. Her solitude was gone.

He caught sight of Dozer, then his blue eyes sought and found her sitting there.

"Are you okay?" he called, his footsteps quickening through the deep grass.

She frowned at him. What was he talking about? "Of course I'm okay. I thought you had files to finish."

He slowed his steps. Obviously, he'd thought she had fallen off Dozer. "I needed a break. I was getting claustrophobic."

Kim felt suddenly grumpy. Of all the trails he could have picked, why did he have to pick the one she was on?

Then she mentally shook herself. She wasn't here just to goof off and spend time by herself, she was here to counsel, and she'd just finished praying for God to use her. Maybe the girls in her cabin weren't the only ones God wanted her to help. She stood up from her seat on the rock and stepped forward to meet her boss.

"You just missed a couple of young deer playing out here. They heard you coming and fled."

He jammed his hands in his pockets, looking dejected. "The story of my life. The only patient I had yesterday fled before I could check her out. Deer flee at the sound of my footsteps." He looked quickly at Kim, then looked away. "Women flee at the sound of my name."

"Am I invited to the pity party?"

He frowned and shot her a look. "You don't believe me?"

Kim raised a brow. "I don't know what Carrie's problem was. The deer would have been stupid not to escape the sound of humans. Women don't flee at the sound of your name, or do

I need to remind you about a woman who followed you all the way—"

"No." He raised a hand to cut off Kim's word flow. He glanced over his shoulder in the direction of the camp. "No jokes about that. It's not funny." He slumped over to the boulder Kim had just left and sat down. "I wish I'd never met that woman." He combed his dark blond hair back with his fingers and sighed. "This was a stupid mistake. I shouldn't have come here."

"Why did you?" She relented and sat down beside him. "You went to a lot of trouble to get the time off."

He glanced at her, then looked away. "I didn't realize. . .I guess I just didn't think." He leaned forward and pulled some thistles from the legs of his jeans. "I had thought this might be a good chance for us to get to know each other better."

"You mean you and me?"

"Is that such a shock?" He shot her an irritated glance, then once again looked toward the direction of camp.

"We see each other less here at camp than we do at the office." And his answer wasn't the whole truth, although Kim knew he was attracted to her. She also knew he'd been a troubled man from the time she first went to work for him, sinking into dark moods, snapping at the nurses.

"The best way to avoid Priscilla Waters isn't out here, alone on the trail," Kim said, and knew from his expression she'd read his mind. "That woman will hunt you down, you know."

He nodded. "Just my luck her brother's the director here. There's no escaping her."

Kimberly smiled. "Use your brain, boss. You like kids. Half your patients are kids. And no one can corner you if you're in the middle of a morning Bible study group or listening to one of Adam's sermons. A group of people makes a good buffer. Just join the activities."

He eyed her suspiciously. "You're still trying to get me *saved,* aren't you?"

"Just a helpful suggestion. You don't have to take it." She stood up and brushed off her jeans. She couldn't believe she was still trying to help him avoid Priscilla, all the way out here in the middle of the wilderness.

He stood with her. "What about the clinic? They hired me to treat patients, not study the Bible."

"Oh, come on, Doss, just use your pager." She whistled for Dozer, and he came, grass falling from both sides of his mouth. "Want a lift back to camp?" she asked Doss. "Dozer won't mind. You'll have to help me on first, though."

A few minutes later, as they rode into the camp, Kim was chagrined to find Adam and Bryson both mounting horses to look for them. She heard Doss groan and looked in the direction he pointed. Priscilla Waters stood at the doorstep of the clinic, hands on hips, glaring at them.

Adam jumped down from Titan. "Where've you been? We nearly called out a search party."

Kim reined in, annoyed. "What do you mean? This is my free time."

"It isn't the doc's," Bryson growled, aiming his pointed stare at Doss. "We have an agitated lady scouring the camp for you."

Doss dismounted. "Miss Waters doesn't look sick or injured to me. What's the problem?"

"Maybe you'd better ask her that question," Bryson snapped. "She thinks, just because she's the director's sister, she runs the camp." He jumped down from his horse and led it into the stable, his dark eyes glowering.

Doss sighed heavily and glanced once more at Priscilla, who did not move from the clinic steps. He turned and reached up to help Kimberly down. "Thanks for the talk, Kim, and for the ride. I guess I'd better go face the music."

Kim frowned toward Priscilla, then shrugged. "Good luck." She felt sorry for him, but he'd apparently gotten himself involved in a relationship that he wasn't finding easy to get out of. She turned back to find Adam unfastening Titan's saddle. "Adam, what's the big idea? Why are Bryson and Waters so upset?"

Adam quirked a curious brow at her. "Isn't it obvious? Bryson's sick of Priscilla Waters and her attitude and demands. She went and found Bryson and told him that you and Doss had left the camp while Doss was on duty and that Bryson had better do something about it, or she'd report the camp to the authorities for not having medical help on-site for all these kids."

Kim felt her temper shoot so high so fast that the hair at the back of her neck prickled. "That woman is wicked," she said, keeping her voice deceptively soft.

Adam shot her another curious glance. "Did you get that news from Doss?"

"Not entirely. Adam, what's she doing here at the camp? How can she be allowed—"

"I'm not the one to ask." He heaved the saddle from the horse, then turned and looked searchingly at Kim. "You're the one who went riding with Doss. Don't you know?"

Kim caught her breath at the sudden, accusing tone of his voice. "No, I don't know. Neither does he. Adam, what's wrong with you? I'm not the one who's been bossing people—"

"Couldn't you have at least ridden separate horses?"

"Sure, if we'd planned to go riding together in the first place," she snapped. "We saw each other out on the trail, and I offered him a ride back. If you and Mr. Bryson and Miss Waters over there want to read something else into it, that's your problem."

His face reddened, and he swung away abruptly and walked into the tack room with the saddle. He came back out seconds later, frowning, shaking his head. "Kim, never mind what I think, or what Bryson thinks; what about your campers? What if they'd seen you come riding in with the camp doctor behind you on the horse?"

"Why would they have thought about it at all?"

Bryson stepped out of the stable, dusting his hands on his jeans. He glanced at Adam and Kim, then looked toward the clinic and shook his head as he walked away.

Kim also looked toward the clinic, where Priscilla and Doss stood outside, holding an obviously heated discussion.

"Looks like I'm not the only one who jumped to the wrong conclusion," Adam said.

Kim looked at him and shrugged apologetically. Maybe if the girls had seen Kim and Doss riding in together, they would have also wondered what was going on. What would Carrie have thought? She'd been told just yesterday why the girls couldn't swim with the boys. Was sharing a horseback ride with Doss any different?

"Okay," she said at last, as she turned to lead Dozer inside. "Sorry, Adam. I didn't think before I offered him a ride. He had thistles all over his jeans, he was unhappy, and I felt sorry for him."

Adam followed with Titan. "I believe you, Kim." He sighed as he reached up to remove Dozer's saddle. "Maybe I'm over-reacting just a little." He handed Kim a currycomb and picked up his own to work on Titan. "You told me Doss isn't a Christian."

"Right."

Adam looked at her and held her gaze for a moment. "And he's just your boss?"

Kim reached up to comb Dozer's back. "Yes."

"You don't have any kind of. . .you know. . .relationship?"

Kim suppressed a smile. "No."

"Okay." There was a tinge of frustration in his voice at her one-syllable answers, and they completed their chore in silence.

It wasn't until they had released the horses and stepped outside the stable that he spoke again. "Kim." He touched her arm, and she turned around to look up at him. "I'm sorry about my. . .uh. . .jealousy. I guess it's an old habit I never outgrew."

Jealous? "That's ridiculous, Adam. You were never jealous of me. Overprotective, but never jealous."

He gave that a moment of thought. "No, you're wrong." He shoved his hands in the back pockets of his jeans and didn't look at her. "It was definitely jealousy I felt when I saw you come riding in a while ago with Doss. It was jealousy I felt when you told me you'd gotten married."

Kim stood staring at him, amazed at his admission, fighting the warm joy that spread through her at the words. Brotherly jealousy. Big deal.

He strolled over toward the fence, where the horses had rejoined the others. "You know, you haven't talked about that anymore."

"I don't like to talk about it." She followed him and leaned against a nearby lodgepole pine. "I told you the basics."

"What did you do after your husband died?"

She grimaced at his inability to leave the past alone. "I didn't do anything different. I already had two part-time jobs waiting tables, and we'd had a small, ratty apartment near downtown KC. I stayed there and eventually got a roommate. After I saved enough money, I left her the apartment and went backpacking."

"The Appalachian Trail. Were you still running away?"

"Maybe."

"Have you come home yet?"

"Maybe."

"You didn't call us."

At her sharp glance, he raised his hands. "I'm sorry; I know we've been through this. It's just that I wish we could have been there for you. I wish you had known you weren't alone and that I didn't want you to be."

She pushed against the tree and stepped up closer to Adam. "I wanted to be alone. I was wrong, and I realize that now, but you know how independent I've always been. I had to find myself helpless, face-to-face with God alone, before I could allow myself to accept His help and the help of His people."

"But it didn't have to be that way."

"For me it did." She put a hand on his arm and grinned up at him. "Jealous, huh?"

His green eyes came alive. He returned the grin, then reached out and drew her against him in a fierce hug. He held her that way for a long moment.

"Um, Adam, aren't you worried about how this might look?"

"Yes." He leaned back slightly. The grin died. He reached a hand up to touch her face, then bent his head toward her.

With a quick catch of her breath, Kim jerked backward, pulling from his touch. For a long, painful moment, they stared at each other in silence. All her life Kim had dreamed of a moment like this. Adam had been the target of all her girlhood crushes and all her grown-up dreams, except for that one time in her life when she'd reached for the wrong thing. That wasn't real. This was.

"Kimberly?" The disappointment and hurt in his voice was real.

"I'm sorry, Adam." What was wrong with her? Was she crazy? "You're too special to me, and I can't do this." She backed away.

He came toward her, hand outstretched. "Why not? Kim, what's wrong?"

"You deserve so much better." With frustrated pain, she turned and fled.

ten

For the next few days, neither Adam nor Kim spoke about their incident at the stables. Kim was too confused about her own emotions to try to interpret them for Adam, and she knew he was embarrassed. When it came to girls and dating and the romantic side of life, Adam had always been shy. Few people were aware of this because his speaking style was so confident and bold, but Kim knew him better than most people. For the next few days they ran together, talked about camp activities, and prayed for the kids, but as though by unspoken agreement, they did not discuss other things.

Carrie stayed out of mischief, to Kim's surprise. Gail was still quiet and sad when she was alone, and Michelle still picked arguments with Carrie, but for the most part, camp activities had an impact on all the girls. They also impacted Kim. The Bible studies taught her to put more of her trust in God, to depend on Him and seek His will more fully. The physical activities and games taught the girls to support each other as a team. They especially liked the exercise in which one member would allow herself to fall backward, and trust the others to catch her. They also liked the "blind faith" test, where one partner would lead the other, blindfolded partner, into the wilderness, guiding each step.

By the middle of the second week of camp, Kim was curious enough, and had worked up enough courage, to confront Adam about the overheard conversation between him and Bryson. As she ran in silence behind him in the early morning darkness, she cleared her throat.

"Um. . .Adam, remember the other day, when Carrie fell into the river?"

"It's not something I'm likely to forget. How's Carrie been behaving since then?"

"I think we're keeping her busy enough that she doesn't have time to get into any trouble."

"Is she getting along with the other girls?"

"Most of the time. Sometimes the practical jokes she and Michelle play on each other get pretty rough. She put ink on Michelle's favorite towel the other day and poured ice water over her in the shower. I've broken up a couple of fights."

"How are Susan and Natalie dealing with it? Do you think it's getting a little rough for them?"

Kim slowed her steps a little as she thought about it. "It gets tough. Sometimes I can't control the language in time, especially when Carrie loses her temper. I've asked Susan about it, and she says it's nothing worse than they hear at public school. Susan especially has a calming force on the others, and Natalie is never shy about talking about God's love and forgiveness. I don't know what I'd do without those two."

"Remember that they were chosen for their leadership skills. This is serious business, Kim. We're trying to reach young, confused kids who wouldn't otherwise be reached." He puffed harder as they ran up a hill. "Keep an eye on Carrie."

"Is she in danger of being sent home?"

Adam reached the top of the hill and slowed to a walk. He turned to look at Kim. "Why do you ask?"

Kim slowed to match his pace. "Because. . .I. . .accidentally. . .overheard you and Matt Bryson talking."

His gaze sharpened and he stopped walking. "When?"

Kim grimaced at his reaction and kept walking. "Don't get bent out of shape, Adam. I wasn't intentionally eavesdropping; it was an accident. I went to apologize to you after I bit your head off. Remember? You were all worried and upset, and I—"

"Kim, what did you overhear?"

"I heard you and Bryson talking in your room—you know, you really ought to be more careful about that; those doors seem to be made of card—"

"What did you hear?" Adam caught up with her and took her arm.

"Well, among other things I heard Bryson saying Carrie would have to be sent home if she caused any more trouble. And I heard you say, in so many words, that you were keeping me out of trouble by running with me in the mornings." She stopped and shot Adam a reproachful glance. "Like now. Do you think I'm some kind of troublemaker who has to be baby-sat to stay out of mischief?"

Adam groaned and covered his face with his hands. "Oh no. This can't be happening. Me and my big mouth." He uncovered his face. "Who else heard this?"

"Nobody else was out in the hall."

"Did you tell anybody?"

"Of course not! Do you think I'm a troublemaker *and* an idiot? What is this, Adam, some kind of undercover thing? You two were talking about a drop of some—"

"Shh!" He grabbed her arm again, glancing hurriedly around the surrounding woods. "Kim, this had nothing to do with you. You weren't supposed to hear anything, and I'm glad you haven't said anything to anyone else." His hand tightened on her arm. "Kim, you've got to trust me on this. You can't say anything. Nothing."

"Don't you think I have a right to hear what was being said about me and one of my girls?"

He shook his head. "I'm sorry, Kim."

Kim stood staring at him in silence for a long moment. "You really don't trust me."

He raised a brow. "Why are you just now getting around to telling me about this? Why didn't you say something last week?"

Kim looked away, embarrassed. What could she say?

"Forget you heard it, Kimberly. That conversation did not take place." He turned and resumed his pace.

She stood looking after him, then rushed to catch up. Fine. Back to small talk.

"We've been so busy with activities, you haven't told me much about how things are going in Eureka Springs. Is the church growing? What's it like downtown now? Has there been a big turnover in the cast at the Passion play?"

A slow smile drew across his mouth, chasing worry from his eyes for a moment as he shot her a glance. "Yes, the church is growing. It's practically doubled in size since you left. Downtown is busier than ever, and the tourist trade is growing. There hasn't been that much of a turnover in the cast, because the actors and actresses see that as their ministry, not just a job."

Kim shot him a sharp glance. She could tell he hadn't meant the words as a condemnation to her, but she still condemned herself. She'd left her part in the play without a word.

"We had a lot of excitement last year," he continued. "There was an attempted murder backstage."

"You mean at the Passion play?"

"That's right."

"What happened?"

"Enid Benjamin—who is now Uncle Clem Elliott's wife—has a niece named Amity. Amity fled to Eureka Springs from Oklahoma City last year because her husband had been murdered. He'd been involved in a crime ring down in the city, and his buddies had turned on him. After hiding out for a few weeks in Eureka Springs, Amity became a member of the Passion play cast and—"

"Whoa! Hold it." Kim raised a hand in confusion. "You're saying Amity was married to a criminal?"

"Yes."

"Was she involved with this crime ring as well?"

"No, Kim." He slowed down and glanced at her. "She made a mistake and married the wrong man, just like you did.

It nearly cost her life and her baby's."

"Her baby's?"

"She was expecting when her husband was killed. The killers thought she knew something, and they traced her to Eureka Springs, all the way to the backstage of the play. A private investigator, who had been hired by Amity's suspicious sister-in-law, saved Amity's life."

"And the baby?"

"His name is Timothy." Adam smiled. "Amity married Titus King before Timothy was born, and together Titus and Amity are finalizing plans for a Christian school just outside Eureka Springs." His smile broadened. "I think they're also hoping for a baby sister or brother to join Timothy."

Kim ran beside Adam in silence for a few moments. "So Amity is a Christian?"

"Yes."

"Was she a Christian when she married the criminal?"

"Yes, she was. As I said, she made a bad decision. We all do that from time to time."

"You don't."

Adam slowed to a near stop. "Kim, how can you say that? Of course I make bad decisions."

"Name one."

He picked up his pace again. "We've discussed it, Kim. I didn't allow you time to grieve over your parents."

Kim stretched her legs to keep up with him. "No, I mean some life-changing decision that was bad, like the ones I made. Adam, you've been a Christian since you were a little kid; you knew you were called to be a full-time minister, and you never wavered. You studied and grew and always knew what God wanted for you in your life." She knew she could never match that. She would always be a questioner. She would always have arguments with God.

"God calls different people to different services," Adam said between breaths.

"But you're so steadfast. Could we slow down a little? I can't keep up."

Adam shot her a teasing glance and slowed his pace. "Steadfast?"

"Pam said you hardly ever dated."

"I still don't."

"See what I mean? You know what God wants for your life, and you—"

"Hold it." He slowed to a walk. He held Kim's gaze for a moment, then looked away. In the dawning light, Kim could see his expression growing more sober. "You sound as if you're putting me up on a pedestal," he said. "I don't belong there, believe me. The reason I've never dated is because I believe there's only going to be one particular person for me to share my life with."

"Yes, but how are you going to know who that person will be unless you get to know—"

"You sound like Mom." His gaze held Kim's more pointedly. "What I'm saying is that there is one person I've always had in mind, and no one else will do." He did not look away, but reached out and touched Kim's arm gently. "I think I have some growing to do before I learn to treat that young lady with the patience and respect she deserves."

Kim stared at him, dumbfounded. "Are you saying you already know who your wife is going to be?"

"I've known for years who I wanted it to be." He hesitated. "When you ran away from home, and stayed away, I had questions and doubts for the first time. I thought God was using this to tell me that you wouldn't be the one."

Kim suppressed a gasp. "Me? You're talking about me?"

He sighed and shook his head. "Haven't you been listening?"

"Yes, but, Adam, with everything that's happened, how can you still—"

"You're back."

"Nothing's the same."

"No, we've both grown, and I believe that was in God's will."

"You're wrong, Adam." Kim couldn't believe she was saying this out loud, and later she would kick herself. "My running away was wrong and so was my marriage. How can you believe that all the rebellion I went through was in God's will? I disobeyed everything I knew to be right. I can't just come back and expect everything to be the same after five years. Neither can you. Nothing is."

"Some things are." He reached out and drew her to him by her shoulders. She allowed him to put his arms around her, and to hold her for a long moment, because that was the one place she wanted most in the world to be. But she couldn't stay there, and tears slid down her cheeks as she pulled away.

"I'm sorry, Adam." She reached up and touched the whisker-roughened skin of his face. "Nothing is the same." She turned and walked away as he stood watching her.

❧

Later that morning, during her free hour, Kim stopped by the clinic to help Doss with paperwork. She'd finished the filing earlier in the week, but Doss was scheduled to do physicals for the campers from underprivileged families, and she helped him keep the records. Her free hour was only half over when she finished typing the last report and glanced up to find Doss tinkering with the x-ray machine.

"Problem?" she asked.

"This thing is so antiquated I can't get it to work right half the time."

"Be glad you've got it. A retiring doc donated it to the camp at least ten years ago, and it was ancient then."

"Where do we take the kids if it breaks down?"

She shrugged. "We can always take them to the ER in Branson."

He shook his head. "That's ridiculous."

"You're just spoiled." She reached for the doorknob to leave, but hesitated. "Doss, are you doing okay?"

He looked up from what he was doing. "Why do you ask?"

"Obviously Priscilla caught up with you the other day when we went riding. You seem even less happy now than when we had that talk, and I would have asked sooner, but you've been busy with physicals. I guess she's still giving you a hard time?"

Doss sighed, sitting down heavily on the desk. "Is it that obvious to everyone?"

"Probably. I've seen her come in here a few times, but there were always kids around. I bet she's getting frustrated if you're still putting her off."

Doss nodded. "She yelled at one of the kids the other day. I told her to shut up and get out." He shook his head. "I heard about that later."

"From her?"

"From her brother."

"So whose idea was it for you to sit with Pam and her campers during worship sessions and mealtimes?" She grinned at him and caught the glimmer of a smile.

"You told me to stay in a crowd. Pam's got a good-sized crowd of girls. I've been taking your advice, and I've attended some of the camp sessions. Don't get your hopes up, but I'm beginning to get a feel of the difference between good and evil." He closed his eyes and sighed again. "Some people are pure evil."

"All of us have that capacity, Doss. Some of us allow it to overtake us. I don't think a human has the ability to generate evil or good all by herself, but she reflects what's in her spirit." She took his silence as a sign that he was listening. "Take Pam, for instance. You can see the goodness flowing from her. That's because she belongs to Christ."

He looked up at her. "And Priscilla?"

Kim shrugged. "A lost soul. We've got a lot of those around here. The wonderful thing is, it's never too late for a soul to find its way ho—"

The doorknob turned in her hand. Startled, she stepped backward in time to see Miss Waters open the door.

"Well, hello," the woman said, sending a mocking glance at Doss. "I believe I heard my name mentioned." She stepped inside, nodding at Kim. Her skintight black exercise outfit clung to her muscular figure, and perspiration dripped from her skin. "I've just had my workout, and I'm hot. Mind sharing your air-conditioning with me?" She sank down onto the exam table, smearing it with moisture. "Don't mind me, you two. Carry on your conversation."

Kim shot Doss a sympathetic glance. "Sorry, but I've got to get ready for a hike." She stepped out the open door, then held it as she glanced at a young teenaged boy coming their way. "I think your next patient is ready for you, Doctor." And thanks to him, Doss would be granted a temporary reprieve from whatever Priscilla was intent on saying.

eleven

Thursday afternoon of the second week of camp greeted Kim
with the joyful prospect of another long hiking expedition, for
which Gail had convinced Carrie to join them. Kim stood at
the stables watching them approach, studying Carrie's expression and the way she interacted with Gail. She could be a good
friend. She could also be a supreme troublemaker when she
was in the mood. Kim hoped she wasn't in the mood today.

As the girls approached, some boys walked toward Kim
from the other direction. Carrie caught sight of them, and left
Gail behind in her rush to intercept the oldest, and cutest of
the boys. Kim glanced at Carrie's shoes—not the sturdy
walking shoes that had been suggested.

"Carrie, don't you have any high-tops?" Kim asked as the
girl drew near.

Carrie stopped and glanced down at her flat, loose loafers.
"These'll do."

"Put some socks on."

Carrie shrugged, grinning at Kim, then at the cute boy,
Derek. "I don't need 'em. I walk all over the place in these at
home."

Kim shook her head and shrugged. "We have several miles
to cover, with uneven trails and some steep climbs."

"Climbing?" Carrie protested, shooting an accusatory glare
at Gail. "You didn't tell me there'd be climbing. I get dizzy
around heights."

Kim attempted to curb her impatience. "Then maybe you
don't need to be going with us. Did you bring your water
bottle?"

Carrie stared at her blankly.

"I have enough," Gail said quietly. "She can share with me."

Carrie shot her a smile. Kim suppressed another sigh of impatience as more young hikers joined them. Several of the kids were dressed almost as inappropriately as Carrie, and several others had forgotten to bring the water bottles Kim had instructed them to bring. For a moment Kim was tempted to leave the slackers behind. It wasn't fair to those who were prepared for a real hike to cut their hiking time for those who weren't. But then, what things in life were completely fair? And they did need to learn to take care of one another.

She decided on a shorter hike with easier trails, something that would give them all a good workout, yet not discourage them from going again. The six-mile round-trip into the hills wouldn't wear them out too much if they stopped to rest occasionally, and the return would be easy.

"Everyone stay on the trail," she announced as she headed toward a familiar trailhead. "And don't lag too far behind. If you get too tired, let me know, and we'll all rest." Her mind was already far up the path by the time she completed her customary instructions and assigned partners.

It was a perfect day for the hike, and after they went around their first curve, they discovered two ground squirrels playing in a patch of sunshine. Farther up the trail, a chipmunk skittered away. Kim raised her fingers to her lips, and for a few seconds, the squirrels were unaware of the presence of the hikers. Then Carrie giggled.

With tails flying, the squirrels scurried up the nearest tree, only to peep around the trunk a moment later, chattering angrily.

The forest was filled with living things. One only needed to know where to look, and Kim explained to the teenagers about some of the surrounding habitat. She had a deep love and understanding of these forests, and her love was contagious. As she talked, more and more of the hikers ceased their chatter and gathered close to hear her words.

They gradually climbed higher into the hills, stopping on occasion for a drink of water or a shoe adjustment—Carrie adjusted more often than the rest. Finally, about two miles in, the echo of running water reached their ears. The sound grew louder as they climbed, until, after rounding a sharp, rocky turn in the trail, they discovered the source.

A huge waterfall cascaded down the side of the bluff, sparkling in the sunlight with thousands of tiny, dancing prisms of light.

Derek, Carrie's main focus of interest for the afternoon, whistled in admiration as his gaze followed the waterfall to see it merge into Kings River far below. "That's cool." He turned to Kim. "This isn't the end, is it? We just got started."

At Carrie's groan of protest, Kim grinned. "Don't worry, I know a secret passage around the falls."

"What?" Carrie exclaimed. "How much farther? I have blisters, and I'm thirsty and my legs hurt, and—"

"Have a drink." Gail shoved her bottle in Carrie's face, showing the first signs of irritation that she had ever shown with her friend. "I think it's a great hike, Kim. How much farther do we get to go?"

"Yeah, Kim, can we go farther?" one of the other kids asked. "This is great. Any more climbing?"

"The next mile will be easy and flat, then we'll turn around and come back. The return trip will be downhill, Carrie, so relax. And if heights make you dizzy, stay away from the edge of the bluff."

As the group rested from their climb, Kim stepped closer to the edge of the trail and gazed out over the valley below. The camp looked small from this vantage point. Kim's old jogging path wound around through the tall trees below the camp. It was the route she had taken the first morning here, when she'd literally run into Adam. She hadn't been there since then because Adam had asked her not to go that way. The road that stretched alongside the trail was empty, as usual. It wasn't much of a road—just two dirt tracks used by the camp trucks when they hauled canoes to and from Kings River.

A movement on the trail now caught Kim's attention. She narrowed her eyes thoughtfully as a human figure detached itself from the trees and moved in the direction of the camp. The figure was too far away for Kim to recognize, but the movements were stealthy. Once, it even jumped back into the shadow of trees, as if the person heard a sound. Instinctively, Kim moved away from the edge. A few moments later, the figure stepped out again.

Curiosity held Kim there. That was the very spot where she had collided with Adam in the darkness nearly two weeks ago, where that strange car had turned off its headlights, as if to keep from being seen.

What was the big deal about that place? Why didn't Adan and Bryson want her jogging down there after dark?

A sudden commotion with the kids jerked her around, and a piercing scream riveted her back to the group. It was Carrie. Again.

"Help me!" came the familiar cry.

Kim raced down the ridge toward the panicked voice, weaving between frightened teenagers. What had that kid gotten herself into this time?

The answer hit her when she arrived at the center of the hovering group, and she saw Carrie dangling off the side of the cliff, holding frantically onto a tree root as she kicked and scrambled to get back up.

Kim dropped to her stomach at the top of the crevice. "Carrie, stop kicking! We'll get you out if you'll be still."

Carrie's face, caught in a grimace of terror, did not register Kim's words. She continued to kick, and pebbles and rocks scattered down the bluff from her frantic activity.

"Carrie!" Kim shouted. "Stop it! You're going to break your hold!" She turned to look up at the kids hovering around her. "Derek, you and Josh grab my legs and hold me. I'm going to try to pull her out."

"Kim!" Gail cried, pushing her way forward. "She'll pull you down too! You'll get killed!"

"Just help hold me." She waited until they had a good grip on her legs, then inched forward on her stomach until she felt she could reach out and grab Carrie's arm. "Lord, help us," she whispered. "Don't let me drop her."

"Hurry!" Carrie cried. "My fingers are slipping!"

"I'm right here." Kim grasped Carrie's right arm with both hands. "Let go of the root and help me pull you up."

Carrie shook her head with a sob, her breath rasping with fear. "I can't! I'll fall!"

"You have to!" Kim cried. "It's the only way I can help you!"

Carrie still didn't release her hold. She dug her toes into the loose, rocky dirt of the cliff. The dirt gave way, and her hands slid farther down on the roots she held. "Help me!"

Kim released her hold on Carrie's arm and grasped her more forcibly around the wrists. "Carrie, remember that talk we had about faith?"

Carrie nodded through her tears.

"Well now is one of those times when you have to have faith in the strength of someone besides yourself. Your life may depend on it!"

Carrie turned wild, frightened eyes up to Kim for a second. Her hands slipped farther.

"Let go!" Kim shouted.

Carrie obeyed. Her full weight came down on Kim's grip. Kim prayed hard and held firm.

"Okay, boys, pull us up!"

Tiny, sharp rocks scraped Kim's stomach as the teenagers hauled her backward against the rough ground. Pain shot through her shoulders as Carrie's weight stretched them in their sockets. Her sweating hands loosened slightly on Carrie's, but then Carrie gave a strong, final kick and shot up over the ledge.

She fell against Kim, and lay panting, clinging to her, tears smearing makeup all over her face.

The kids helped them farther away from the cliff edge and surrounded them, helping Kim to her feet. Kim reached down to help Carrie.

"Ouch!" Carrie cried, stumbling. She slid back to the ground with a grunt. "I can't stand up," she said, wiping her face with the back of her sleeve.

Kim sank to her side. "What's wrong?"

"It's my ankle." Carrie reached down and grabbed at her leg. "I can't stand up. It hurts. It really hurts!" Fresh tears began.

Kim examined the offending left ankle, which had already begun to swell. "What happened?" She looked up at Gail. "How did she fall?"

The girl shot Carrie another irritated glance. "She stumbled."

Kim could guess the rest. Carrie had been flirting with Derek, trying to get his attention—trying to get everyone's attention—and had stepped too close to the ledge.

"I should have been watching," Kim said as she examined the ankle again.

"Is she going to be okay?" Derek asked.

"We'll need to get her to the doctor and have her ankle x-rayed," Kim said. "We'll have to figure out a way to get her back to camp. No more hiking today."

There was a collective groan.

"Way to go, Carrie," one of the kids complained. "If it weren't for you, we'd be past that waterfall by now."

"Yeah, Carrie. You didn't even bring your own water."

Kim saw the stricken look of pain that crossed Carrie's face.

"Be quiet," Gail warned them. "She wasn't the only one who didn't bring water or wear the right kind of shoes."

"So how are we going to get her out of here?" Derek asked Kim.

"By horse." Kim studied the group of teenagers, amazed by her own stupidity. Why had she brought such a large bunch of kids out here without another adult? Now she'd have to leave them up here while she went down to camp and brought Dozer back up.

She stood to her feet and dusted off her jeans. "Who wants to go with me?"

Several raised their hands, including Gail. But Kim didn't want Gail leaving Carrie. She chose a couple of athletes to go with her and left orders for the others to stay put and keep an eye on Carrie.

She prayed silently as she led the others in a rush downhill. *Lord, please don't let Carrie's ankle be broken.* Bryson would probably send the girl home, and that would break Carrie's heart.

"Can you believe Carrie?" one of the girls muttered behind Kim. "She'll do anything for attention."

"She's sure getting it," another replied. "First the rapids with the canoe, then this. Next time she'll kill herself or somebody else."

Kim frowned, picking up the pace. The trail curved around trees, past small creeks. Sweat dripped from her forehead. Running with hiking boots was a lot different from jogging along a flat surface with athletic shoes, but as long as those with her didn't complain or fall behind, she kept up the pace. Her boots felt like logs tied to her feet by the time they reached the stables, and Kim was very glad to see Dozer in the paddock.

She told her companions to check in with their group counselors, then stepped into the tack room. The tangy mixture of leather, soap, and horse sweat combined to greet her. She pulled Dozer's huge, lightweight saddle out, threw a blanket on top, along with the bridle, and carried the load to the corral fence.

Dozer greeted her eagerly, and she was soon riding him back up the path she had come. He moved with unaccustomed speed, and she imagined it was because he sensed her urgency. Probably, he was just bored and needed a good run, but whatever it was, she appreciated it.

They arrived at the cliff about forty minutes from the time Kim left, according to her watch. She saw Carrie sitting on a rock with her foot propped up, with the rest of the teenagers scattered along the trail on boulders. Only Gail sat talking to Carrie. The water in her bottle was gone.

Carrie's eyes grew larger and larger as she watched Kim draw close, astride Dozer.

"I'm not ridin' that thing!"

"Yes, you are." Kim hopped down and moved to Carrie's side. She bent down and probed the offending ankle. "How does it feel now?" She noticed a little more swelling than it had shown before, so much that the shoe was tight, where before it had been loose.

"It hurts."

Kim probed a tender spot.

"Ouch!" Carrie stiffened. "Is it broken?"

"We'll find out." Kim directed Derek and Jason to lift Carrie onto the horse.

"No!" Carrie stared at Dozer fearfully. "I can't ride that thing, Kim, I told you! I've never ridden a horse before."

Kim bit her lip and said nothing for a moment. She'd risked her life to save this kid's hide twice; she'd put up with her mouth and her attention-seeking antics for two weeks. She was getting tired of Carrie. Maybe it would be best if Bryson did send her home. Then maybe the whole camp would be more peaceful.

She looked down to find Carrie watching her.

"You're going to make me do it anyway, aren't you?" Carrie asked.

"Yes."

To Kim's surprise, the girl didn't protest further. "Will you ride with me?"

"Yes."

Carrie hesitated a moment longer, then raised her arms. "Okay, guys, haul me up."

Suddenly, Kim found herself suppressing a smile as the boys gently lifted and placed Carrie onto the saddle on Dozer's broad back.

Carrie gasped and held tightly to the saddle as Kim climbed on behind.

"Are you sure this is safe?" the girl croaked.

"Safer than swimming the rapids or dangling from a cliff," Kim retorted. She put her arms around Carrie and took the reins. "Okay, let's get back to camp."

The two of them rode in silence for a few moments, listening to the chatter of the hikers who followed them. Carrie gradually relaxed. A few moments later, she turned her head and grinned up at Kim.

"This ain't so bad, is it?"

"That's what I've been telling you," Kim said. "Maybe when you get better you can come riding with me, if the doctor releases you."

Carrie's pretty blue eyes widened with alarm. "What's gonna happen to me now?"

"They'll x-ray your ankle, and if it's broken, Doss will set it and put a cast on you. Then all the boys can sign it. How would you like that?"

"Do we have to go to the doctor?" Carrie asked. "Maybe we can just wait and see. Maybe we can splint it, or go to the cabin and put some ice on it and wait."

Kim sighed. "What don't you like about Dr. Carpenter?"

Carrie shook her head and didn't reply.

"He's a good doctor, Carrie. I've worked with him. I know. Besides, we have to make sure there isn't a break. You don't want to go through life with a limp, do you?"

Carrie shook her head again. "I don't want to see that doctor."

Kim didn't say another word, but when they reached camp,

she guided Dozer to the infirmary.

"No," Carrie whispered.

"Take her down, boys, and get her inside," Kim said, sliding to the ground. She ignored Carrie's beseeching look and turned to walk through the open office doorway.

Doss sat at his desk with his back to the door.

Kim knocked and entered. "Hello, Doc. Our accident-prone camper is here to see you, and this time she's not getting out of it."

The boys filed in behind her with Carrie.

Doss frowned at Carrie. "I see. Has our swimmer been at it again?"

"It was a cliff today," Kim said. "Thanks, guys," she told the boys who'd helped her. "Until next time." She glanced across to see fear evident in Carrie's expression, then looked back at Doss, who watched the girl with an uncertain wariness.

"Could you check her left ankle, Doss? She can't put any weight on it."

While he checked out the patient, Kim watched the two together. Carrie was stiff and jumpy, and even Doss continued to be uneasy. Kim shook her head in frustration. Whatever their personality conflict, they would have to work it out themselves. There was work to be done, other kids to see about.

Doss straightened to face Kim. "Our machine is broken again. I'll have to take her into Branson."

"But I thought you used it yesterday on one of Pam's girls."

Doss turned and picked up a set of car keys from his desk. "I got one shot out of the thing before it quit on me. We'll probably be a while, so don't look for us to be back soon. I'll just go to our office in town, instead of trying to get into the emergency room. I'll bring the car around."

When the door closed behind him, Carrie turned frightened eyes to Kim and grabbed her arm with both hands. "Kim, can't you go with us?"

"I'm sorry, Carrie, but I've got other responsibilities. You'll be okay. The x-ray won't hurt, and Dr. Carpenter is one of the gentlest doctors I know."

"But—"

Doss stepped back inside. "Let's get this patient to the car."

Carrie shrank back from him when he reached for her. "Kim, please. Come with me."

"Nonsense." Doss lifted Carrie into his arms. "Kim has other things to do. Let's get out of here."

Between them, Doss and Kim settled the patient comfortably onto the backseat of the car. As Doss drove away, Carrie turned and stared out the back window at Kim, and Kim saw tears in the girl's eyes.

twelve

A rude nudge snapped Kim to attention, and she whirled around to look up into the indignant dark brown eyes of Dozer. He nudged her again. Kim laughed. Dozer snorted and stomped his foot.

"What's the matter, boy, haven't you been getting enough attention?" She rubbed his nose. As she did so, it occurred to her that someone might come looking for Doss while he was gone. She stepped into the infirmary, found a piece of paper and a pencil, and jotted down a short note to leave on his desk.

When she turned back toward the door, she found Dozer standing in the threshold, his huge head jutting through the open doorway. He obviously didn't intend for her to get away from him.

"Okay, okay, let's get that nasty old saddle off and give you a long rubdown." She pushed him backward out of the opening and turned to pull the door shut behind her. When she turned back around, she saw Adam coming toward the infirmary from the staff quarters.

An instinctive smile crossed Kim's face. "You're a little late," she called to him. "I could have used your help a couple of hours ago."

He returned her smile, though the smile didn't reach his eyes. He looked worried about something. "Why is that? It looks like you just had a good ride."

Kim turned Dozer around and headed him toward the stables. "Surely you've heard by now about Carrie's accident."

The smile slipped from Adam's face. "No. What happened?"

"Where've you been? The news must be all over camp by now."

103

"What news, Kim? I've been on the phone since lunch. We're missing a camp director, and until he decides to reappear, I'm it."

"Mr. Waters is missing?" Kim exclaimed.

"Yes. Kim, what happened to Carrie?"

"She fell and hurt her ankle on our afternoon hike. I had to come and get Dozer to carry her down out of the hills."

Adam glanced toward the infirmary. "How is she doing?"

"She's scared right now. Doss had to take her into town to do the x-ray, because the machine's broken again."

Adam stared at Kim in shock. "Doss drove her to Branson?"

"He had to. There wasn't any other way—"

"Did anyone else go with them?"

"No."

"How long ago did they leave?" he demanded.

"I don't know, maybe about ten minutes. Doss is taking her to our office instead of to the emergency room."

With a sudden look of panic, Adam whirled toward the parking lot. "Keep an eye on things for me, Kim. And tell Bryson what happened!"

"But where are you going?" she shouted after him.

Without answering, he disappeared past a stand of trees. In a moment, she heard a car start and saw Adam pulling out of the camp.

With a shake of her head, she turned back to take care of Dozer. It seemed the longer camp continued, the stranger things got around here. There were too many mysteries.

Fifteen minutes later, she left Dozer contentedly rolling in the sand. The girls wouldn't be finished with their afternoon activities for another hour, which left Kim plenty of time to do a little exploring. She didn't intend to break her promise to Adam. She would not be leaving camp property, and she was not exploring after dark.

Back at the cabin, she changed quickly from her jeans and hiking boots to a pair of lightweight sweat pants and running shoes. If anyone saw her, they would naturally assume she was out for an afternoon jog, which she was. Another one.

She remembered at the last minute that Adam had commanded her to inform Bryson about this afternoon's circumstances. With a quick glance at her watch, she stepped out of the cabin and rushed to the camp offices, adjacent to the lodging for the ancillary staff. The secretary did not know where Bryson was, so Kim left a message with her. That would have to be good enough.

She left the buildings and chose the most shady pathway down to her old jogging road. She ignored the guilty suspicion that she was breaking someone's rules somewhere. Like Carrie, she was sick of rules and of the secrecy and close-mouthed distrust she'd seen in Adam and Bryson.

From the cliff, just before Carrie's fall, Kim had seen someone down on the road. Recalling how visible that figure had been, she hugged the line of trees whenever possible and hurried toward the place where she and Adam had collided that first morning, almost two weeks ago. Why had he been down there in the first place, so early in the morning, when he'd complained every morning since then about having to get up so early to exercise with her? Kim wished she could turn back time and replay that scene. Surely she would have noticed something, seen something that could give her a clue about what was going on.

When she reached the tiny path that connected the trail to the road, she stood looking up and down the trail. This was still camp property, as far as she knew. None of the trail maps included this, yet it was very well worn. Who would be hiking this area regularly enough to keep the brush pressed back and the spiderwebs cleared? She hadn't taken a group down here, and she was the only designated trail guide at camp.

The narrow median separating the trail from the road was thick with trees and dense brush. The trees used to completely overhang the narrow connecting path. No longer.

Someone had cut the largest of the branches. Where weeds and grass had grown, there was now bare dirt on the trail. Kim bent down and studied the footprints. There were several different shoe marks, but none looked like they had been made by the sole of a hiking boot.

Kim straightened. So what? She wasn't going to prove anything hanging around down here. She took a few cautious steps through the dark green stillness out to the road, where numerous sets of tires had cleared the growth away in a double track. She bent down again and discovered what looked like three sets of footprints superimposed over the latest tire marks. This was the approximate spot where she had seen someone from the cliff. She straightened and shaded her eyes to study the bare, sandy-white glare of the bluff above and to the south.

She saw the waterfall and the water-darkened rock beneath it. She was proving nothing down here, except for the fact that this remote area was seeing a lot more traffic than it used to when Kim attended camp every year.

Still curious, she turned and jogged back the way she had come. Adam wasn't about to tell her anything. He didn't trust her. He'd already taken great pains to keep her away from here. If he knew she was here now, he would probably panic, although he hadn't actually told her to stay away from this spot during the daytime, had he? He was only worried about her coming down here in the early morning darkness, which was one reason he ran with her.

So what went on down here in the dark?

Just as she reached the end of the trail and caught sight of the first cabin, a faint noise pricked her ears. It was an airplane. This triggered the memory of airplanes she had heard when she was lying in bed, once in the early morning and once late at night before she fell asleep.

She also remembered the car without headlights. What if she did her jogging earlier than usual some morning, and did it alone?

Shouldn't she just trust Adam? She should leave this whole thing alone.

But what could it hurt just to check things out? She knew how to stay out of sight. She wouldn't be causing any trouble. She was curious.

"Hey!" came a voice from the steps of the lodge.

Kim's thoughts scattered, and she jumped around to find Pam walking toward her.

Pam grinned unrepentantly. "Sorry, didn't mean to scare you. I guess you know I'm beginning to develop an inferiority complex around you. Just what are you up to, anyway?"

Kim hesitated. "What do you mean?"

"Are you trying to win the Heroine of the Year award? I guess if disaster has to follow poor Carrie around, it's a good thing you're there to pick up the pieces."

Kim relaxed. "I suppose that means you've already heard about the accident on our hiking trip."

Pam fell into step beside Kim and they walked toward the cabins. "Everyone knows by now. You know how fast news travels around here. How's Carrie?"

"I don't know yet. Doss had to take her into Branson to x-ray her ankle because our machine isn't working. I just pray the ankle isn't broken, because if it is, the director might ship Carrie home." If they could find the director.

"Why would they do that?" Pam asked. "She can use crutches. It might slow her down a little, help keep her out of more trouble."

Kim shot her friend a rueful glance. "I think it's the 'more trouble' they're probably worried about."

"Do you want them to send her home?"

"No."

"She's a handful."

"Yes, but isn't this camp for kids like her?"

Pam raised an inquiring brow at Kim. "Then all you have to do is say a few words to Doss."

"What do you mean?"

"He's the camp doctor, right? And the camp doctor has always made the medical decisions before." She smiled, as if to herself. "They'll listen to him. He has a way with people."

"Oh, yeah? He doesn't have a way with Carrie. Those two don't seem to get along very well."

"That doesn't matter," Pam said with a shrug. "He'll still listen to you."

"What makes you so sure about that?"

"He likes you. I mean, he *really* likes you. I know firsthand because without any encouragement from me, he's begun sitting with our group at mealtimes."

"So I've noticed."

Pam shrugged her plump shoulders. "I think he sits there because he knows you and I are friends, and he just wants to talk about you."

They stepped up onto the concrete porch of Pam's group cabin. "Do you ever get a chance to talk to him about God?" Kim asked.

"Oh sure, I slip things in between his monologues about how efficient you are at work, how well you seem to get along with the kids, how he admires you for working during the day and attending school at night." Pam opened the door. "I wouldn't mind hearing a man talk about me like that. Especially a man like him."

"Watch it, Pam," Kim warned. "I told you; he's not a believer."

"He can have a change of heart, especially here at camp."

"Then pray for that. I know there's always hope, so pray for him."

"Believe me, I am."

&

Gail barged through the cabin door ahead of the others, barely a minute after the camp bell dismissed the afternoon activities. "Is she okay? Did they x-ray her foot? Is it broken?" she asked, rushing up to Kim. The rest of the group clamored behind her.

"Wait a minute; don't trample me!" Kim exclaimed, holding her hand in the air. "We don't know anything yet. Dr. Carpenter had to drive her into Branson to x-ray her, and I don't know how long they'll be gone."

"It's all my fault," Michelle moaned, slumping elegantly down onto her bed. "I dared her to go. I said she was such a sissy, she couldn't keep up."

"It wasn't your fault," Natalie assured her. "Gail said she was goofing off too close to the edge of the cliff."

"Yeah and besides," Joni told her sister, "she just went so she could flirt with the boys."

"She got her wish," Gail murmured. "They helped her onto the horse, then carried her into the infirmary."

"So you see?" Natalie said brightly, "Carrie will say it was all worth it."

Kim smiled as she stepped out onto the front porch to watch for the car. Natalie was probably right. So why worry?

Her worry, in spite of mental reminders not to, jumped to new proportions when Adam did not return for the evening praise service. Three of the counselors did a great job substituting, but Adam had been scheduled to lead the service. He'd arranged for replacements, but he hadn't returned. Kim didn't see Mr. Waters, the director, either.

The evening stretched out interminably, and Kim grew more concerned by the moment. She left the girls chattering back and forth across their beds, and strolled over toward the hillside to watch the darkening sky. The cool evening breeze felt good against her skin, and she tried to relax in the influence of the serene quiet surrounding her. She'd almost convinced herself not to do any more snooping down at the road, but now her curiosity had reached new heights. An extra jog earlier in the morning wouldn't hurt her, and she hadn't actually promised Adam that she wouldn't go without him, had she? No, she had not promised.

To Kim's relief, a car drove by the cabin a short time after Kim had turned out the lights for bedtime. She jumped quietly out of bed, pulled on her sweats, and let herself out the cabin door, careful not to disturb the sleeping girls. She moved quickly through the darkness, and reached the infirmary just as Doss opened the front passenger door to help Carrie out.

"What happened?" Kim asked. "What took you so long? How's the ankle?"

Doss pulled out a pair of crutches from the backseat and held them for Carrie, whose ankle was wrapped in an elastic bandage. "She's going to be fine," he said. "No broken bones. If she uses these crutches and stays off the foot," he emphasized, pointing his finger sternly at the girl, "she should be better in a couple of weeks."

"Then I'll have the rest of the girls take turns sitting on her," Kim said.

Doss grinned at Carrie. "I think that's a good idea."

Carrie stuck her tongue out at both of them and returned Doss's grin.

Kim leaned against the car. "It's good to see you two are finally friends."

Doss nodded. "Yes, it is, especially since Carrie keeps needing medical attention." He gave Kim a few instructions, then said good night.

Kim adjusted her stride to walk beside Carrie. "I hope you're not too tired to tell me what happened tonight. What took you so long?"

"Haven't you ever gotten stuck in Branson traffic?"

"There are back roads."

"Not to the doctor's office. After the x-ray we went and ate." Carrie yawned noisily. "Oh, yeah, Adam came and talked to Doss for a long time while I waited, but I didn't hear what they were talking about."

"So when did you and Doss become buddies?"

"After Adam left, Doss and I talked."

"Oh?"

Carrie glanced at Kim, but didn't explain. She just nodded. "Yeah, we're okay now."

thirteen

The soft beep-beep of Kim's alarm woke her instantly the next morning. She groped around the in the dark, found her watch, and switched it off before it could rouse any of the girls—though at four-thirty in the morning, she doubted anyone would stir. Rubbing her eyes sleepily, she pushed back the covers.

Clamping her jaw to silence suddenly chattering teeth, she pulled out the bundle of warm, dark-colored jogging clothes she had stuffed under her bed last night. While she pulled them on, she glanced at Carrie, whose face was illumined by the glow of an outdoor light that filtered through the window. The girl looked so young and denfenseless with her features relaxed, her makeup removed. With relief, Kim thought again about the change in Carrie's attitude toward Doss. Whatever had happened between them, it was a good thing.

Kim stuffed her pajamas beneath her pillow and pulled on her jacket. Would there be time for a nap later today? She would need one.

With slow, stealthy movements, she opened the front door. A few days ago, she'd taken care of that squeaky hinge so it wouldn't squeak. It slid back in perfect silence, and the latch made no noise as the door shut. Of course, it wouldn't have mattered if one of the girls had awakened because they were used to Kim's early morning treks. Still, she didn't want to take unnecessary chances this time. She crept across the main campground. Adam mustn't find out that she'd even left the cabin. She probably shouldn't be doing this. No, she knew she shouldn't be doing this. She was going to do it, anyway. The curiosity would kill her otherwise.

When she reached the trees, the cover of darkness gave her a feeling of security, which she was beginning to need. This was a stupid thing to do. Maybe even dangerous. The silence hung like a blanket over the hills, and Kim knew she had to step with caution. She felt the need to hurry, however, so she increased her pace as much as she could without breaking the silence.

Something rustled in the brush nearby.

Kim stopped and pivoted around, her heart pounding. Had someone followed her? She tiptoed over toward the shadows beneath some trees.

The underbrush rustled again, and Kim relaxed slightly. It was something small, like a chipmunk or a squirrel. She waited a few more seconds. A cat ran out of the bushes and crossed through the camp. It didn't even glance at her.

By the time Kim arrived down at the road in the valley, she couldn't tell if her quickened heartbeat came from exertion or fear. Both, most likely. Nothing moved as she peered into the woods. No sound reached her ears. No one had arrived yet, if anyone was even planning to come.

Satisfied that she had not been seen, she stepped into the tangled growth of woods and peered into the murky darkness.

A huge, dark shape loomed ahead of her, and she stopped, stifling a gasp. A few seconds later, as her eyes grew accustomed to the gloom, she recognized the shape as a thick growth of bushes she had seen yesterday. Perhaps those bushes would even provide a good hiding place for her. She crawled into the shadows and settled herself amongst the overgrown pokeweed and buckbrush, wondering how long she would have to sit here in this cramped position.

The crackle of a nearby branch answered her no more than ten minutes later. Without turning her head, she glanced toward the trail. The dark form of a man came strolling toward her. Thank goodness she'd arrived so early!

She tensed as the man entered the connecting path. Could

he see her? Of course not.

He stepped to within inches of her crouched form. Sweat beaded her brow. The blood pounded in her ears, and she swallowed hard. He walked past her toward the road a few yards away, and Kim was sure he could sense her presence, hear her breathing or her heartbeat. She had almost convinced herself that he was waiting for her to give herself away, when she heard the faint sound of an automobile coming along the road. As before, there were no headlights.

The car came steadily closer until it finally stopped beside her dark visitor. He stepped over to the car, and Kim strained her ears to hear over the low purr of the motor.

"What happened last night?" he asked the person in the car.

Kim stifled a gasp. That was Bryson's raspy voice; she would recognize it anywhere!

"Breakdown in communication somewhere along the way," a man from the car answered. "They said they'd have it fixed by tonight, though, so be ready for the pickup at our regular time." The man paused. "Was the boss mad?"

"Very."

"Are the phone lines still bugged?"

"We can't tell for sure, so don't even try to call. Don't fax or E-mail, either. We can't take any chances," Bryson said. "Now get out of here before it gets light."

"Okay, but if something goes wrong tonight, don't blame me," the man replied as he pulled away.

"I *will* blame you," Bryson called after him softly.

Kim froze as Bryson turned and retraced his steps along the path. He walked a little way, stopped, and turned to watch the car disappear. Silence descended again. Bryson didn't move. It was as if he were listening, was aware of Kim's presence, and was waiting for her to make the first move. The moments crept by slowly. Something rustled in the brush along the edge of the road, and Bryson stepped toward the road. Kim waited.

To her amazement, Bryson chuckled softly. "What are you

doing here, cat? Spying on me?" He bent over, and Kim watched him pet the same cat that had startled her up on the hill. "Just don't come sneaking up on people like that anymore, okay?" He straightened and walked along the connecting path to the trail, back the way he had come.

Kim expelled a shaky breath. What if the cat had sniffed her out and called Bryson's attention to her? Or what if she'd made a noise? The man obviously had excellent hearing.

As badly as she wanted to get back to the safety of her cabin, she forced herself to wait a few minutes longer before she moved. When she decided Bryson had time to get all the way back to the lodge, she straightened and stepped out onto the path. She stood a few moments in the silence, but heard nothing. She had to get back. She turned and crept down the path. A pine branch caressed her hand, and she jumped, muffling a cry.

Her thoughts raced wildly as she picked her way through the shadows to the jogging trail. Interesting how something so familiar and comfortable to her could change in such a short time; the once-friendly trees now loomed menacingly over and around her.

What had she done? If Bryson had caught her, he could have done anything to keep her quiet. And who was the boss? The way the men had talked, it sounded like someone at the camp. It wasn't Adam. It couldn't be. She felt as if the tentacles of this unwelcome mystery were drawing her in far deeper than she wanted to be, but what could she do? What was going on?

The first greeting of the morning reached her ears when an early rising songbird decided it was time for everyone to wake up. The normally happy sound jarred Kim. This was not a happy morning. Whatever Bryson was doing, Adam was obviously involved too. Kim had known Adam all her life. From her first memory of him, she had only known him to be good and honest. Oh, sure, there'd been the usual, boyish mischief, the pranks, the practical jokes and teasing, but nothing evil in any way. Adam had been the stabilizing influence Kim needed when her parents were killed. She had always admired his strong convictions, even when she wavered herself.

Adam was not capable of treachery. So what was going on? She couldn't just come right out and demand that he tell her what he was up to. She'd already tried that. He wouldn't tell her. He might even make her leave. The way she saw it, if she wanted to know what was going on, she had no choice but to return to her hiding place tonight and wait for the next scene to unfold.

She reached the crest of the hill and stepped from the trees. The camp still rested in darkness. She reached the cabin shadows just in time to step back out and greet Adam as he came to meet her for their morning jog.

His eyes were a little more bleary than usual. "Morning," he growled.

"Good morning, Adam," she said brightly. "And how much sleep did *you* get last night?"

He rubbed at his unshaven face and scratched his head. "Not enough."

"That couldn't be because you spent the evening chasing all over Branson for Doss and Carrie, could it?"

"Nope."

"Oh, that's right." She studied his expression. "They got back long before you did."

"That's right." He continued to plod along in silence for a moment, then he raised a brow and looked at Kim, a trace of a smile finally lighting his green eyes from the glow of his flashlight. "You noticed?"

"Of course I noticed! How could I keep from noticing, when you went tearing out of camp yesterday, frantic about Doss and Carrie, ordering me to tell Bryson what was going on?"

The smile grew. His pace picked up. "Worried about me, huh?"

"Yes. You worry about me all the time, so I thought I'd turn the tables for once."

"How does it feel?"

She increased her pace to keep up with him. "Sinful. Worrying is a sin, right, Adam?"

"Sure is. It's also a common human failing. You're human."

She shot him a frown. "You already know how human I am. Did Mr. Waters return to camp?"

Adam's smile wavered and fell. "No."

"Has he called?"

"No."

"Are you still trying to find him?"

Adam slowed a little. "Of course we are, Kim, but his car is gone. It looks as if he left on his own. He seemed a little strange to me, anyway." The pace slowed even further, and Kim was relieved. "I'm not sure about him."

"What do you mean?" Kim asked. "He's the camp director. Didn't that screening committee check him out before he took over as interim?"

"Yes, and I even interviewed him over the phone. He had excellent recommendations, and he impressed me when I spoke with him, but he was different in person. He was quiet, he kept to himself, and when I asked him if he'd lead the staff in a special Bible study, he declined."

"And he's gone now. What about his sister, Priscilla? Is she still around?"

Adam spread his hands. "We can't find her either." He glanced at Kim, then closed his eyes and shook his head. "I shouldn't be talking about this, Kim. I'm sorry."

"I asked."

"Yes, but I didn't need to burden you with all this. If I'd kept my mouth shut last night—"

"Would you stop being so hard on yourself?" Kim grinned. "You're the acting director now, you know. I think you'll make a great one. Remember what you always told me—trust

God to be in control, and stop trying to play God."

The lines of worry slowly eased from his expression, just as the sun warmed the morning air and lifted the darkness around them. He glanced at the early beams filtering in through the trees, then looked at Kim. "You know what, Kimberly Bryant? I like you." He reached over and took her hand, squeezed it, then let her go. His voice softened. "You know what else?"

She read the words on his face like a blessing, but she couldn't let him say it. She raised her hand to his lips and shook her head. "I like you, too, Adam Patterson." And she loved him. And she knew he loved her. He didn't have to say it, and the knowledge gave her a confusing mixture of joy and pain. "And it's time to get back to camp." Without waiting for his reply, she turned back along the trail and broke into a run.

The girls were still sleeping when she stepped back inside the silent cabin and closed the door. She leaned against it and gazed down at their faces. They looked so innocent and serene, so unaffected by life's tragedies. But Kim knew better. Some of them had suffered pain she couldn't imagine. What would it be like to have to give your baby up for adoption? How would it feel to have to raise yourself because your mother was busy working and your father didn't care enough to stay around and see you grow up? When her mom and dad were alive, they loved Kim and remained active in her life. Michelle and Joni felt unwanted by either of their divorced parents.

She clapped her hands. "Time to get up, ladies!" She gave Carrie's good foot a quick tickle. "That means you too, Carrie. Don't think just because you're momentarily handicapped that you can get out of the praise service this morning."

The girl shot her a surprisingly warm smile and yawned noisily. "Who says I wanna miss church?"

"Huh?" Gail muttered as she rolled over in bed. "That you, Carrie?" She rubbed the sleep from her eyes and stared at her friend. "Carrie! Your ankle. . .it isn't broken?"

Michelle pulled the covers down from around her chin and glanced over toward Carrie. "So you're still alive. For someone who doesn't like the doctor, you sure see a lot of him."

Carrie grimaced. "Who says I don't like the doctor?"

One by one, the girls crawled from their beds and crowded around Carrie, their excited chatter mingling into a confusion of sound. Kim left them talking and went into the bathroom to shower. The stinging needles of water pelted her skin as she brooded again over the long morning she'd already had. She should have told Adam. She felt guilty about sneaking out the way she had. The problem was, she still planned to do it again in the morning, and if she told Adam about it, he would stop her.

Why couldn't she just tell him and trust him to take care of things?

Because too many suspicious things had been happening. The big problem was that he would not confide in her. He didn't trust her. Would he even listen to her if she warned him to be careful and told him about this morning?

He wouldn't talk, so she wouldn't either. Did he even suspect, as she did, that Waters's disappearance could easily have something to do with the rest of the mystery? If he did, he hadn't told her. And that was the big problem. She'd felt their lack of communication stifle their spirits when they prayed together in the mornings.

Kim poured shampoo onto her hair and scrubbed vigorously. She needed to think about her girls. They were the reason she was here, and she was so encouraged by Carrie's sudden change in attitude. She was still Carrie, of course—impulsive, loudmouthed, flirtatious—but now some softness was counteracting the belligerence. It was probably always there, and she'd just relaxed enough here at camp for it to show.

After rinsing, Kim turned off the water and reached out to grab a towel, sending up a silent prayer of thanks for Natalie and Susan. In just two weeks, they had shown the depth of their Christian faith and their eagerness to share Him with others.

Drying herself quickly, Kim waded through the fog to her robe and slipped it on. She used her sleeve to wipe some of the steam from the mirror, then combed the tangles from her hair.

The bathroom door opened and closed behind her, and an arctic blast of air hit her legs.

"Kim?" came a small, tentative voice from behind her.

Kim peered through the mirror to see Carrie standing there, large eyes watching her.

"Yes, what's wrong?"

The girl limped forward. "Tell me again what a Christian is."

Kim turned to face her. "A Christian is someone who realizes she can't avoid sin on her own and turns to Jesus Christ as God's only Son, who died as payment for those sins."

"But what if she sins again?"

"She continues to have faith that Jesus will take those sins away and keep her from wanting to sin." Kim studied the girl's thoughtful expression. "Does that make sense to you?"

Carrie braced herself against the wall and hobbled closer to Kim. "Well," she said hesitantly, "I know what faith is now. I learned the hard way." She grinned up at Kim, then sobered. "If I hadn't trusted you to get me over that ledge and hadn't let go of that tree root believing you'd save me, I might still be hanging on up there. . .or dead." Her expressive eyes widened at the thought.

"And?" Kim prompted.

"Is that what it's like with Jesus? Are we just supposed to have faith that He'll save us from death?"

"Yes," Kim replied, excitement leaping within her. "Ever heard anybody say, 'Let go and let God'? You let go of your hold on your own life and give it over to Christ. Then He pulls you out of the pit of sin."

Carrie bit her lip. "Kim, I'm really sorry for everything I've done, all my life. I don't want to be that way anymore."

"Do you want to put your faith in Jesus to save you?"

Carrie's chin quivered. She held Kim's gaze steadily. "Yes. I do have faith." She took another halting step forward and leaned into Kim's outstretched arms. "I believe!"

Tears of joy stung Kim's eyes. She pulled Carrie back slightly and smiled down on her. "Don't you think you should talk to Jesus about it?"

"You mean pray?"

"Ask for His forgiveness and accept Him as Lord."

Carrie stared at her. "Out loud? Right now?"

"Are you afraid?"

"Kind of. I mean, this is God we're talking to. It's like, He's the King, you know? Of the universe."

"He's also your Father—like a loving daddy—who loves you more than any earthly father could ever love you."

Carrie continued to stare at Kim. "I don't know what that's like," she said softly.

Kim stared back at her in shock. Of course she didn't know. Her father had never been around. "Give Jesus a chance to show you, Carrie. He won't let you down."

Carrie prayed then, a simple, short prayer that came from her heart and brought tears to Kim's eyes. After the prayer, she looked up at Kim again.

"God really does answer prayers, doesn't He?"

"Yes, Carrie, He does. My prayer now will be that your new faith will go with you when you leave camp."

"Mine too."

"Mine too!" Natalie's voice echoed from the doorway, and all the girls rushed into the bathroom to surround Carrie.

Due to the circumstances, they arrived late for morning praise, and Adam was already speaking. Kim listened to his deep, comforting voice, watched the earnest sincerity in his expression, and felt overwhelming tenderness and love for him. She forced herself to listen to the verses he read and the words he spoke and pressed down the guilt she still felt about keeping this morning's secret from him. She also said a quick prayer for help with her worry. What if he got hurt? Was he in danger already? She couldn't bear it if something happened to Adam. Again, she forced herself to listen to the message God revealed through him. The message was about trust.

When they were dismissed for breakfast, the rest of the campers rushed from the auditorium with their customary lack of reserve. Kim's group followed more slowly so Carrie could keep up with them on her crutches.

"What a perfect day!" Carrie exclaimed as she hobbled beside Kim.

"You're absolutely right," came a voice from behind them. They turned to find Adam walking their way. "I know why it's beautiful for me," he said, his gaze resting on Kim. "Why is it beautiful for you, Carrie?"

She told him as they filled their plates and sat down, and the genuine joy he showed made Carrie glow. It also kicked her chatter into high gear as she spoke about the witness Kim had been to her and what she'd learned in the past two weeks about faith in God.

Halfway through the meal, to Kim's surprise, Priscilla Waters appeared at the entrance. Kim and Adam both stopped eating and watched her cross the cafeteria toward Doss, who sat with Pam and her group. She leaned forward and spoke a few words to Doss. He shook his head and turned away. She bent closer and whispered something in his ear, then turned and stalked out. Doss slowly put down his fork and followed, his face turning pale.

Kim leaned toward Adam. "Did you want to ask her about Mr. Waters?"

"I already did. She arrived before services this morning. She says she doesn't know where he is."

Kim shook her head. "Well, isn't she worried?"

"Nope. She says he does stuff like that all the time." He shrugged and spoke into Kim's ear. "I guess I just used bad judgment."

"Miss Waters is gorgeous," Michelle murmured a few moments later. "I wish I looked like that. Did you see those clothes? She's a bodybuilder, you know. And her hair—"

Carrie turned suddenly and glared at Michelle. "You don't know anything about beauty. She's ugly." She paused. "She's evil."

Kim stared at Carrie in surprise.

The girl turned her head back toward the entrance, then tapped Adam on the arm. "Will you help me back to the cabin? My ankle's startin' to hurt. I want to lay down for a while."

Adam nodded and rose to his feet. "Take your time," he told Kim. "We'll be okay. I'll get some ice from the ladies in the kitchen."

When Kim and the girls returned to the cabin thirty minutes later, Adam met them at the door. He laid a hand on Kim's shoulder. "We need to talk. Now. Let's take a walk." He turned to the others. "Watch Carrie for us, please, ladies. Don't let her put any weight on that ankle."

Kim followed him, mystified, several yards along a nearby forest trail. "Adam? What's wrong? What's going on? Do you think Carrie's ankle is worse? Maybe we should ask Doss—"

He stopped and turned to her. "It's not that." He studied Kim's face for a moment, then hesitated, looking away, then back at her. "Kimberly, do you trust me?"

Uh-oh. He knew! "Uh, yes."

"Enough not to ask any questions right now?"

"About what?"

He rolled his eyes and shook his head, then laid a hand on each of her shoulders and squeezed gently. "I need some help from you, but I can't explain why right now. Please trust me."

She held his green gaze for a long moment, then nodded.

He emitted a short sigh of surprised relief. "Good. I need

you to keep watch over Carrie constantly. Don't let her out of your sight, and don't leave her alone with any other adult, even someone you trust. Would you promise to do that for me?"

Kim frowned. "Okay, Adam. It makes sense to me. I think you're being a little overprotective just because Carrie is a klutz and you don't want her sent home. She needs to stay here at camp for the support right now."

He grinned and shook his head. "That's not the half of it. Thanks, Kim. I owe you."

Before she realized what was happening, his hands tightened on her shoulders. He bent forward and kissed her, a short, unrehearsed, and very sweet kiss. Then, with his face turning red, he turned and led the way back to the cabin.

fourteen

"Okay, everybody, listen to me," Kim called out across the cabin to her chattering group of girls. "Tomorrow is visitors' day, and we want to make our parents proud of us, don't we?"

"Like how?" Gail asked.

"We're going to have a cleaning session this morning before we do anything else."

"Oh, come on," Joni grumbled. "It looks okay."

"Hush," Michelle snapped at her sister. "There's mold growing in the bathroom. Our parents probably won't be here to see it, but somebody will. Cleaning will be good for us."

"Cleaning?" Carrie complained. "Cleaning." She glanced down at her wrapped foot, and a slight smile touched her lips. "What do I get to do, supervise?"

"First, you'll make out a slip of paper for each job that is to be done, then you'll fold them, and we'll each draw one until we're done," Kim told her.

Carrie grinned. "I can handle that."

"After that, you can do the lower windows while I do the uppers." At the look of feigned outrage that crossed Carrie's face, Kim burst into laughter. "Let's get started."

The cabin was soon a whirl of activity. Michelle scrubbed the baseboard while Gail dusted. Susan and Natalie scoured the bathroom with pine cleaner. Joni helped Carrie with the lower windows and swept the front porch. They opened the windows to let the fresh air blow through, and Carrie started singing a praise song—off key. Soon, with a pained expression, Michelle joined her just to get her on pitch, and the others helped until they developed a beautiful three-part harmony.

As Kim sang and polished the last of her windows, she

caught sight of Adam walking out of the lodge with Priscilla Waters holding his arm. Kim nearly lost her balance from the chair on which she stood. She stopped singing as an uncommon surge of jealousy struck her speechless for just a moment.

Below her, Carrie stopped singing too. "Hey! What's goin' on out there?" She stood up to get a better view. "What's Adam doin' with that woman?"

"What woman?" Michelle demanded, rushing to the window to see what Carrie was talking about. She caught sight of Adam with Priscilla and gasped. The others joined her.

After a moment Kim smiled to herself and resumed polishing. "He's not doing anything but talking." He was still looking for Priscilla's brother, and he obviously thought she knew more than she'd told him this morning.

Kim grew suddenly aware that the girls had fallen silent and were watching her, all except for Carrie, who continued to stare out the window at Adam and Priscilla with obvious resentment.

"Would you guys relax?" Kim said as she replaced the chair and moved to put the cleaning supplies away. "One thing I have learned about Adam is that you can trust him. I've known him all my life."

Michelle shrugged. "What's not to trust? I mean, you're not going steady with him or anything, are you? And he's walking right out in the open with her."

"Stop it, Michelle!" Carrie snapped. "Adam shouldn't go out with a woman like Priscilla Waters. Besides, he loves Kim. Everybody can see—"

"Okay, time to get everything put away," Kim said quickly. "I'm proud of you all. We've surely got the cleanest cabin in camp." She glanced at her watch. "It's almost time for craft classes, so let's finish before we're late."

Later, Kim went to sign up for activities for the visitor's weekend. To her chagrin, she discovered that Matt Bryson was in charge. He surprised her by agreeing to allow her to take a group on a float trip down Kings River, then he gave her strict time restrictions and take-out points. His dark eyes held hers a little longer than was comfortable, as if he were trying to read her thoughts. She glanced away quickly. Could he guess about this morning?

As she stepped outside again, she heard Pam's voice calling to her from the infirmary door. "Hey, skinny britches, what're you doing at the lodge?" She closed the door and strolled casually toward Kim.

"Come walking with me and I'll tell you," Kim suggested as they met in the middle of the clearing. "I think I have visitors' day planned."

Pam followed Kim downhill toward the river's edge. "Aren't John and Kate coming to see you?"

Kim thought with affection about Adam's parents. "Yes, but I can't spend the whole day with them. Besides, they could come with us if they wanted. We're going on a float trip down Kings River." Kim stepped over a pile of rocks and accidentally stepped into soft mud.

"Leave it to you to come up with something fun like that," Pam said. "We're going on a nature hike. I could sure use you as a guide. You know all the trees and plants and animals."

"Not all of them. Besides, chipmunks and squirrels and birds aren't hard to figure out."

Pam shrugged. "At least the camp siren will be gone by tomorrow."

"What's that?"

"Sorry, I'm being catty. Priscilla Waters is planning to leave this afternoon. I saw Doss helping her load her car with some suitcases."

"I'm surprised she's stayed this long. She doesn't seem interested in our activities."

"No, but she likes one particular person quite a bit." Pam looked so dejected that Kim stepped over to her and laid a hand on her shoulder.

"You have a crush on Doss, don't you?"

Pam glanced quickly at Kim, hesitated, then sighed. "Yes. You did warn me to be careful."

"I'm sure you have. You're too logical to become involved with someone just because you are very attracted to him. We'll pray about it together, okay?"

"How about now?" Pam asked with a grimace. "I could really use some help."

As the two women grasped hands and bowed their heads, Kim prayed aloud. She soon heard Pam sniffing and felt tears slide down her own face. It had always been like that between them; when they prayed together, they shared their doubts and pain and tears, then felt the healing power of the Spirit soothe them. A few moments later they finished, looked up at each other, and smiled as they dabbed at their wet faces. Nothing had changed.

꿔

Kim changed her mind several times about her spy trip that night. It wasn't until the girls went to bed thirty minutes earlier than usual that she decided she was going to try it. She dressed once again in dark clothing, pulled her long bright hair beneath a scarf, and pulled the covers back over her pillow.

Her stomach tightened as she tiptoed out the front door and pulled it securely shut behind her. A nearly full moon peeped over the line of trees, and the dark sky held a heavy scattering of stars. No clouds covered them. Kim took short, shallow breaths as she stepped off the cabin porch.

She continued to concentrate on her breathing as she hiked downhill to the place from which she had watched Bryson this morning. This place had seemed forbidding to her this morning, but tonight it looked monstrous. She had to suppress a shudder and force herself into the shadows. In the midst of the clump of bushes where she would hide, she sank to her knees, praying silently that she would be concealed through this escapade. She tried not to think about the fact that she hadn't consulted God about this adventure.

After settling, she listened attentively through the tiny sounds of the night for any rustle or footfall, anything that might alert her to an approach. The night sounds grew louder. A frog croaked from somewhere nearby. A sharp breeze passed through, making the limbs and bushes rustle and groan. Kim's muscles tensed at the sounds, but nothing happened. She wished she had the freedom to press the tiny button that would illumine her watch, but she didn't dare move now. Someone might already be waiting in the depths of the forest, watching and waiting, just as she was.

Even as she thought about it, another sound reached her ears. It was distant. . .the rumble of an engine. As it came closer, Kim realized it didn't sound like a car engine. It was an airplane.

At the same time, she sensed movement along the path in front of her. She froze in shock when she realized that someone actually had come quite close while her attention was on the airplane. The figure, dressed again in dark clothing, wore a ski mask tonight. She still recognized Bryson's sense of fluid movement and the catlike bulk of his body. Two more figures joined him this time, both dressed as he was, and Kim felt a quick rush of relief when she realized neither one was Adam. These people were shorter than Adam. She just hoped he didn't join them on the trail.

The inevitable fact was, though, that even if he didn't appear for this particular scene, he was obviously involved.

Branches crackled and the tangy scent of cedar grew stronger as the dark figures crushed leaves and needles beneath their feet. They stepped past Kim, only a few feet away, and though she knew she was well hidden, she stopped breathing for a moment. The airplane descended until it barely missed skimming the tops of the trees along the road. Just as it reached their position, a dark bundle came crashing down through the trees to land several yards up the road.

Bryson darted out onto the brightly moonlit road as the airplane flew away into the night. The diminishing rumble was quickly replaced in Kim's ears by the furious rushing of her blood. She watched in growing shock as the figures on the road bent over their delivery.

Bryson said something Kim couldn't hear, then he lifted the bundle with a heavy grunt and carried it back beneath the trees. Kim bit her lip. The thought suddenly occurred to her that she would now have to take this plan a step farther if she wanted to see what was in that shipment. She would have to follow them. Could she do that? Did she really need to know?

Bryson's two companions glanced around warily as they followed him back into the shadows, stepping closer to Kim. She froze, taking short, quiet lungfuls of air as they approached her.

"Wait," one of them whispered, catching up with Bryson. "Check it and see if it busted open in the fall."

The three of them did a quick check while Kim held her breath.

"It's okay," Bryson whispered. "Let's go!" He hoisted the burden higher and strode forward once more. Kim trembled with relief as they stepped past without glancing in her direction.

Her relief ended quickly when the plastic-wrapped bundle caught on a sharp branch that protruded from the bush behind which she crouched. The plastic tore, and several smaller packages scattered onto the ground before Bryson noticed.

"Watch it—it ripped!" he exclaimed. "Help me get them picked up. Fast!"

The other two scrambled to the ground and felt around in the darkness for the pieces of plastic. One of the searchers drew closer to Kim, and she held her breath in terror. One groping hand came to within inches of her left knee, and she grew dizzy with fear and lack of oxygen. Any moment someone would see her, sense her presence, and—

"We've got them," Bryson said gruffly. "Let's go."

As the small group stole up the trail and disappeared into the night, Kim clamped her jaws together to silence her chattering teeth. Even when she couldn't hear them any longer, she stayed where she was, all determination to follow them having fled during her near discovery a moment ago. Besides, their accident had made it unnecessary to risk detection further.

Crouching in the darkness as she had been for so long, she'd had time for her eyes to grow accustomed to it. She had seen, as the others had not, that one of the packets had landed in the middle of the thicket behind which she hid.

She waited a few moments longer, then inched her right hand between the slender branches of the bush. She grasped the package firmly, then stood to her feet. Nothing stirred around her. Even the frog had stopped croaking. Kim stepped out from behind the bush and crept down the trail, darting constant glances around her to make sure no one returned.

She reached the cabin without detection and slipped inside without waking the girls. Silence remained uppermost in her mind while she slipped off her shoes and tiptoed past her innocently sleeping girls into the bathroom. Filled with dread over what she would find in the package, she stepped to the sink and leaned over it. With trembling hands, she lifted the dark green plastic-wrapped package to the light, then lowered it to the sink. Drawing a steady breath, she tugged on the tough plastic until it gave way. Several smaller packages, wrapped in clear plastic, tumbled into the sink. Kim froze. They contained white powder.

Tentatively picking up one of the packets, she recalled a few nightmare times from her marriage when she had seen packets just like this. This looked like the drugs her husband used to buy from "friends" who came to visit.

With shaking fingers, Kim opened the packet. She tipped a tiny dosage into her open palm, then wet the tip of her finger and dipped it into the powder. She touched it to her tongue, then frowned.

It couldn't be.

She took a larger fingerful and tasted it again.

The dusty-dry sweetness was unmistakable, yet she couldn't believe it. Why all the secrecy? Why the smuggling? This mysterious package before her, for which she thought she had risked her life, was plain powdered confectioners' sugar.

fifteen

Shadows moved across Kim's vision. The chop-chop of a helicopter pounded in her ears. The leaves in the trees sprinkled her with moisture, but her attention was caught and held by the bundle that descended slowly. . .slowly, to land on the ground beside her and scatter into pieces.

"Kim! Oh, Kim! Get up, sleepyhead!" The bed shook, and Kim squinted her eyes open to find Michelle leaning over her, sprinkling water in her face with a wicked grin. "It's time to get ready."

Sunlight filtered through the trees and through the window near Kim's bed. She groaned and sat up with the dawning knowledge that all the girls were awake and moving around the cabin.

"What time is it?" she asked groggily.

"It's exactly ten minutes after eight," Carrie said. "Didn't you tell us our visitors will start coming at nine?"

The words soaked into Kim's sleep-muddled brain. Her eyes widened with shock. She yanked her covers back and leaped out of bed. "Oh no! Why didn't you wake me?" she cried as she grabbed her towel and raced for the bathroom. She was back in five minutes, showered and shampooed and wondering about Adam's reaction to being stood up on the jogging trail this morning.

The girls teased her mercilessly about oversleeping as they walked out of the cabin together, ready to meet their visitors. Natalie and Susan had known their parents would not be coming today because they were out of state, leading a marriage enrichment seminar. Natalie and Susan had volunteered to help with name tags, and they walked toward the lodge through a

133

growing crowd of people who flocked in from the parking lot. Gail's parents had promised to be here, as had Carrie's mother. Kim was concerned about Michelle and Joni. Although their father had told them he would come, they held little hope that he would follow through because he had failed them too many times before. When the two sisters shrieked and raced through the crowd toward a man in a three-piece suit, Kim was overjoyed. Carrie and Gail went off in different directions, waving and smiling.

Kim did not see the people they greeted, however, because she suddenly caught sight of Adam coming toward her. With him were his parents, John and Kate Patterson.

Kim caught her breath and stared at them. For her, the sounds and sights of the other arriving visitors disappeared. The feelings of warmth and comfort flowed through her as she rushed forward to greet the people who had taken her in as their own. John's tall frame and short salt-and-pepper hair looked as it always had, and Kate's fair-skinned, golden-haired beauty had not aged. They looked wonderful. But Kim stopped as the memory of the past few years haunted her suddenly. How could they ever forgive her for what she had done to them? Why had they even bothered to come here? Had Adam told them anything, or would she have to brace herself to see their shocked and sorrowful faces when she shared her recent history with them?

They continued to walk toward her, the joy of greeting on their faces. As they drew near, Kate held her arms out, and Kim no longer hesitated. She rushed forward into Kate's embrace. John and Adam joined them and they all hugged for a long moment in silence. Kim did not cry as she had that first morning at camp, but the wonder of her acceptance by these loving and kind people struck her forcefully. She could not speak, but only smiled and hugged them again.

"I'm so sorry," she said at last with an emotion-tightened voice.

"Sorry?" Kate asked in wonder, her green eyes—so much like Adam's—kind and loving. "You can't imagine how happy we are to see you! Adam has told us so many good things about you, about what you're doing with the girls here at camp, about your church work in Branson, and about your college." Kate took a step back, and placed her hands on her hips. "By the way, Kimberly Bryant," she said with that forceful sense of timing that Kim suddenly remembered so well, "you will take your college money out of the bank and use it for school. No arguments; it's simple common sense."

Kim shot Adam a look of reproach, which was greeted by a broad, unrepentant grin. "What else did you tell them?" Kim demanded.

"He mentioned the hike," John said, his deep, gravelly voice full of approval. "It didn't surprise me at all. You've always been the kind of gal who isn't afraid to tackle a challenge." He leaned closer again, placing an arm back around Kim's shoulders. "Kind of like that little teenager in your cabin you introduced to Jesus."

Kim darted another glance at Adam as she realized that she couldn't continue to bask in the innocent approval of her foster parents.

She cleared her throat self-consciously. "Um, Adam only told you the good stuff, didn't he?"

Kate shook her head. "Have you ever known him to sugarcoat anything?"

"But—"

Kate placed her fingers over Kim's lips. "Don't worry. Our son didn't come tattling to us about every single little thing you've done the past five years. He told us how you've suffered, and I can tell he's very proud of you the way you've persevered. Someday we'll talk about everything else, but does it really matter to us right now? Nothing's going to change the way we feel about you, so let's spend this precious time together just getting to know one another again. Okay?"

Kim smiled and nodded.

"And we've got another surprise today," John said as the four of them strolled downhill toward the river's edge. "Titus and Amity King are here with their baby, Timothy. I know how you love babies, Kimberly. Titus and Amity are working with Clem and his new wife, Enid, to build a Christian school at the edge of Eureka Springs. They want to check out this camp, see how the program is working, mixing troubled kids with those from stable Christian homes. What do you think, Kim? Are the kids doing okay?"

Kim hesitated, shooting Adam a glance of warning.

Adam ignored the look and spoke for her. "Kim feels she's a bad influence on the kids, but I think the evidence, and the girls themselves, might tell you a different story."

"The setup is a good one," Kim said, cutting Adam off with another warning glare. "I just wish we had more than six weeks with these kids. Carrie is a Christian now, and I know that will have a powerful impact on her life. The problem I see is that when she goes back home and falls into the same routine running with the same friends, she's going to have a lot of temptation and no support from us except through letters and phone calls."

"That's where our follow-up plan is implemented," Adam said. "Our staff has already contacted Christian youth groups from the surrounding area where Carrie lives, and some of them will come here for visitor's day in a couple of weeks. They'll meet Carrie, take part in the activities, and give her some foundation for new friendships when she gets back home."

"And whose idea was this?" Kate asked.

Kim raised a brow and gestured toward Adam. "His."

"Not entirely," he said. "Kim voiced the concern during our morning prayer time—which, by the way, you missed this morning, Kimberly."

"Sorry. I overslept."

"I waited for at least thirty minutes. I didn't want to wake the girls up, so I finally gave up and ran by myself."

"Well, you poor thing," Kate teased. "I can see you two still get along as well as any brother and sister."

Kim felt Adam's sudden focused attention on her. She refused to look at him.

"We get along better than we ever have," Adam said softly.

Kim looked up to find John and Kate smiling gently at her. Oh, brother, this was getting sticky. If Adam would just keep his big mouth shut. . .but that was too much to be hoped for, and she knew it. Adam had always been very open and forthright about everything, just like his parents. Kim had been like that once too. Now, there seemed to be so many things about which she must be silent.

It occurred to her suddenly that she had forgotten about Adam's request that she not allow Carrie out of her sight.

"Uh-oh, Adam. Carrie—"

"It's okay. She's with her mother." This time, he did not look at his parents or elaborate. They did not ask questions.

A few moments later, the four of them returned to the center of the campground and, to Kim's relief, found Carrie and her mother, Chloe, chatting with Mrs. Morgan, the talkative kitchen volunteer. Gail arrived with her parents in tow to meet Kim and Adam.

Carrie's mother did not seem perturbed at Carrie's crutches, and Kim had no trouble explaining about the accident. Chloe just waved her hand dismissively and said, "If it's breakable, Carrie'll break it. She takes after me."

Kim was delighted when all the parents entered into the spirit of the day with enthusiasm. She watched her charges show off the crafts they had worked on for two weeks, then behave with decorum and respect during the worship service. John and Kate listened to their son's sermon with joy and parental pride. Halfway through the service, Kate glanced sideways at Kim, and the older woman's eyes filled with tears. She smiled and hugged Kim and whispered, "I'm so glad you're home, my dear. You don't know how much we've missed you and prayed for you. Our prayers have been answered."

Kim felt her own tears smart her eyes. "So have mine."

Lunch that day was served outside on the picnic tables because the cafeteria couldn't hold the increased population in one sitting. Rather than stand in the long line to wait for their food, Kim and her group, including parents, decided to change clothes at the cabin before they ate. It worked. By the time they returned to the picnic area, the line had disappeared and they were served immediately. Because space was short, Kim and Chloe, Carrie's mother, ended up sitting a table away from the rest. This gave Kim the opportunity to explain about Carrie's newfound faith.

"I'm glad you got to come today," Kim said as she placed barbecued roast beef between two soft slices of bread. "Your daughter has been a blessing to us these past two weeks."

The woman, who had short black hair much like Carrie's, snorted with laughter. "Lady, you've got the wrong mom. I'm Carrie's mom, remember?"

"I'm aware of that," Kim said quietly. "Carrie is special, and I think you'll find some changes in her when she gets back home."

"Oh, yeah, the crutches." Chloe took a big bite of her sandwich and grabbed a swig of soda to wash it down. She chewed a moment, then swallowed. "Done that before. We've been through lots of stuff you don't even know about." She started to take another bite, then shook her head. "I didn't expect this place to change her into a new person. To tell you the truth, I needed the break. That kid runs me ragged. I'm sure glad I don't have four just like her, or I'd be dead by now and that loser who's her father would be doin' his share of the kid raisin'." She took another bite of her sandwich.

"She is full of energy," Kim agreed. "She's smart. She can really make something of her life if she's channeled in the right direction."

"Oh, yeah? Are you sayin' you can do that in six weeks, when I haven't been able to do it in sixteen years? How old are you?"

"It isn't me," Kim said. "I don't have anything to do with it. Carrie is a Christian. She's like a new person. Oh, she'll always be Carrie, impulsive and full of life, but now she has Someone else to live for besides herself. She's—"

Chloe held up her hand. "Hold it, Kim. I know you mean well, but I gotta tell you, I don't believe all that stuff. You can say my kid's changed, but that don't make it so. I've gotta see it for myself." She took another swallow of soda and gestured toward her daughter at the other table. "You don't know the trouble that kid's caused. I'm just about to give up on her and let the state take over."

Kim stared at the woman.

"What can I do?" Chloe asked. "She don't mind me, don't listen to me. She ran away from home last year and then got involved with a drug ring, and I don't have the time or the money to go runnin' all over the state looking for her. Don't get me wrong; I love Carrie, but you don't know what she's put me through."

Kim could imagine. She felt sorry for Chloe, working two jobs to support herself and her daughter. With God's will, Carrie's new attitude would stay with her to the point that even her skeptical mother would soon notice the difference.

"You think I'm horrible, don't you?" Chloe asked.

Kim reached over and touched the woman's arm. "No, I don't. I'm sorry you've had to go through so much, and I have seen in the past two weeks how strong-willed Carrie can be. Please, just give her a little more time."

Chloe stared back at her. "Why do you care? If you've seen how bad she is, why would you worry about her?"

"She's changed. Let her prove it. We'll be keeping in touch after she goes home next month. I'll give you my telephone number and address, and you can contact me if you need to.

I've become close to Carrie, and I really want to know how she's doing."

The woman shrugged as she folded her paper plate in half and moved to get up from the table. "Whatever. I'm Carrie's mother, and I have to love her, but she's a real problem."

Kim gathered her trash and followed. "Just listen to Carrie this afternoon," she said. "I think you'll like what you see."

The rest of the group joined them, and together they walked toward the boat dock. Before they reached it, however, two strangers caught up with them. The man had dark brown hair and green eyes, and he carried a baby. The woman's long chocolate-brown hair nearly reached her waist, and the expression of joy and contentment gave her delicate, well-defined features a special beauty.

"Kim," Adam called. "Come and meet Titus and Amity King. And this," he said as he lifted the baby from the man's arms, "is Timothy."

The baby smiled and reached out toward him, and Kim stood watching, enchanted. She greeted the parents, and looked again at Amity's happy smile. "I've always loved children," she told the woman. "Babies, especially. He looks like both of you."

Titus reached over and hugged his wife. "Yes, he does, doesn't he?"

Amity took a step closer. "Kim, I've heard a lot about you," she said softly. "Your family is so happy you're home again."

Kate came forward and put an arm across Kim's shoulders. "Amity's in our prayer group in Eureka Springs," she explained. "She knows how we've been praying for you, and she knows about God's answer to our prayer. Titus plays Peter in the Passion play. Amity was invited to play Mary Magdalene last year, but she's found other things to do with her time." She grinned at Timothy and laughed when he grinned back.

"I don't blame her," Kim murmured. "If I could have a baby

like him—" she caught herself and glanced at the others. "Sorry. He's just so beautiful. Are you going canoeing with the rest of us?"

"Timothy and I are staying behind," Amity said, then looked at her husband with such a wealth of love that Kim watched them both, entranced. "You go, Titus. I know you love float trips."

A few moments later, Kim found herself pushing the others off in their canoes and walking back to a shaded sitting area to join Amity and Timothy. They played with the baby that afternoon, and Amity told Kim about the experience last year when her husband was killed. Then she told her more. Kim was amazed by Amity's openness when she talked frankly about the abuse she'd suffered at the hands of that man before he was murdered, about her foolish decision to pursue and marry the wrong man in the first place, and about her fears when she discovered she was carrying his child.

Kim shook her head. "Titus treats him like his own."

Amity leaned forward and held Kim's gaze with unwavering sincerity. "Titus loves Timothy as his own, and he loves me with a love I never deserved. I am so blessed, even after I blew it the first time."

"Your late husband was a member of a crime ring?"

"Yes, in Oklahoma City. I knew nothing about it at the time, but I should have been discerning enough to know what he was before I married him." Amity paused as she checked Timothy to make sure he was sleeping. "He was an alcoholic."

Kim watched the baby sleep for a moment, then turned and watched the river currents as they eddied near the dock. This woman, who wasn't many years older than Kim, had a loving husband, a baby, and was building an exciting future. She, too, had messed up her life, and God had given her a second chance.

"Amity, how much do you know about my past?"

Amity shrugged. "I know about your parents," she said

with quiet sympathy. "I'm sorry."

"You know I ran away from home, probably, but you don't know the rest."

"What's important is that God knows."

"I was married, too. My husband was a drug dealer and a thief. He was shot and killed robbing a store."

Amity's face showed none of the shock Kim had learned to expect whenever she told someone. It only showed empathy.

"You remind me of myself last year, Kim."

"I bet you didn't run away from home and eat out of trash cans and steal food."

Kim saw the tender expression that entered Amity's eyes. "Forgive yourself, Kim. I couldn't forgive myself for a long time, and I knew I was unworthy of Titus and his love. Titus was pure and good. I felt dirty and worthless. When he found out I was carrying my dead husband's baby, he managed to convince me that he was the right one to help raise the baby, the same way Joseph helped raise Jesus. It's taken a long time, though, to accept the fact that no matter what I feel I deserved, God had better things in store for me than I ever dreamed possible." Amity reached out and gently touched Kim's arm. "He has that in store for you too. Learn to forgive yourself, Kim. God has already forgiven you." She glanced down the river, the way the canoers had gone. "I think Adam has, too."

sixteen

For the remainder of visitors' day, Kim noticed Carrie and her mother talking a lot, often stepping away from the rest of the crowd for privacy. She prayed for them, and she asked Kate and John and Adam to pray with her. She was encouraged when Chloe drew her aside just before leaving camp.

"Carrie's been tellin' me about you this afternoon, Kim. I owe you an apology, and a lot of thanks. You saved Carrie's life twice. Maybe after all that you really do know what I've been goin' through with her."

Kim smiled. "No, I don't. You've been her mom for sixteen years. God just used me to show Carrie what faith is all about. Now she understands."

Chloe shrugged. "Well, I don't know about faith and all; I just know what Carrie's said."

"Then I hope you keep listening to her when she gets home because she'll be telling you all about that faith. She has four more weeks here to learn more about it too, and what she learns will follow her wherever she goes. Would you do something for me?"

Chloe nodded. "You name it, lady."

"Will you make sure Carrie gets to go to church, and will you go with her?"

Chloe stared at Kim for a moment, then nodded. "I'll try." She squeezed Kim's hand quickly, walked over and hugged Carrie good-bye, and joined the other parents in their tired but happy trek back to the parking lot.

Kim said her own good-byes to John, Kate, and the King family, then turned and joined her girls on the way toward the cabin.

"Oh, Kim, can we go on another float trip next week?" Natalie burst out. "That was so much fun!"

"We'll ask," Kim said, glancing at Natalie and Susan. "Was today a little rough on you two, since your parents couldn't come?"

"No," Susan replied. "We knew they had that conference this weekend. We know they'll be here next time, and they'll be so happy to see us when we get home—"

"That's easy for you to say, Susan," Michelle cut in as she stepped up to the cabin door. Tears filled her eyes and slid down her cheeks. "You've never been through a divorce." She shook her head as her sister's tears joined her own. "You don't know what it's like. Our parents will never come together to see us because they hate each other's guts." She looked down at her sister. "Sometimes I think they hate ours too." She whirled around and burst through the cabin door and into the bathroom, with Joni following her.

They shut the door forcefully behind them, and Kim and the others heard heartbroken sobs echoing from the other side. Tears of sympathy welled up in Carrie's eyes, and she stepped toward the bathroom door. Kim put out a hand to stop her, but then she hesitated, and followed her in.

The sight of the two girls sitting on the edge of the tub and clinging to each other tore at Kim's heart. She knelt down between them and reached out to stroke each bright head of auburn hair. Her throat ached with unshed tears of sympathy as the girls leaned against her and cried harder. What could she say? No words of comfort came to her. How could she know what Michelle and Joni were going through?

Several minutes passed, and the sobbing gradually quieted until all that was left were dry hiccups. Hugging both girls to her, Kim continued to search for the right words.

Carrie hobbled forward. " 'The Lord is my shepherd; I shall not want.' "

Kim glanced up to see tears slowly trickling down Carrie's

cheeks as she struggled to recall the Scripture they had been learning in Bible class.

" 'He maketh me to lie down in green pastures; He leadeth me beside the still waters.' " She hesitated. "Um. . .'He restoreth my soul; He leadeth me in the paths of righteousness for His name's sake. Yea, though I walk through the valley of the shadow of death, I will fear no evil: for Thou art with me. . . .' " She stopped and looked at Kim, her blue eyes troubled. "I forgot the rest."

" 'Thy rod and Thy staff, they comfort me,' " Michelle continued for her, a shaky smile replacing her tears. " 'Thou preparest a table before me in the presence of mine enemies—' what enemies?" she asked. "Joni and I are surrounded by friends. 'Thou anointest my head with oil; my cup runneth over. Surely goodness and mercy shall follow me all the days of my life: and I will dwell in the house of the Lord forever.' " She stood up to hug Carrie.

The tears had dried.

☙

A little later, as the girls prepared for bed, Kim went for a stroll. Peace and stillness permeated the camp, and the grounds were mostly quiet while all the different groups gathered in their separate cabins and shared thoughts about the day's events. She sat down on a log near the infirmary and didn't realize she was not alone until a voice spoke.

"I have something to tell you." It was Doss, standing in the doorway.

Kim looked up at him in surprise, then scooted over and patted the place beside her. "Let's hear it."

He strolled over slowly and took the place she offered. For a moment he didn't speak. When he did, he asked about Carrie.

"She's doing well," Kim said with a smile. "Very well. I'm happy to see how you two got along. She's changed a lot these past couple of days."

Doss glanced sideways at her. "Do you think it might have something to do with the way I've changed, as well?"

Kim noticed his warm smile. "What do you mean, Doss?"

"Adam followed Carrie and me into Branson the afternoon she sprained her ankle. While Carrie waited, almost patiently, Adam and I had a long talk."

Kim was afraid to ask. "About what?"

Doss shrugged. "About whether or not to keep Carrie at the camp. About you. And about my relationship with Christ."

Kim caught her breath. "I didn't think you had one."

His smile widened. "I do now. Adam introduced me in a way I'd never been introduced before and taught me about repentance and forgiveness in a way only he could have done. I see things so. . .differently now, Kim. I may have to go through a lot of hardship before I come out on the other side, because I've gotten myself involved in things I should never have done, but I've given it all up." He fell silent for a moment, then sighed. "You know, Kim, I was jealous of Adam when I first arrived here. I knew deep down that he had something special to offer you that I didn't have. I saw the way you two treated each other, and I knew how hopeless my. . .attraction was to you. Now I know what that special something is, and I have it too."

"Doss, I'm so happy for you!" Kim gave him a quick hug, then hesitated. "That wasn't the only reason Adam followed you to Branson, was it?"

"No, it wasn't." Doss took a deep breath and glanced down at his hands. "He was worried that I had taken Carrie away from the protective confines of the camp. He had good reason to doubt me—not that I'd ever hurt Carrie." He glanced at Kim, then away again. "There are some things that I still can't talk about—not for a while yet—without breaking trust with some other people."

"I understand." It frustrated her, but she understood, kind of. She just wished she understood more.

When she returned to the cabin, she wished she had understood a lot more. She was greeted by six horrified faces and open drawers with scattered belongings.

"Kim, someone's been searching through our things," Michelle announced in a quivering voice.

"Yeah," Carrie said, folding T-shirts and putting them back in a stack. "You know how Natalie's always so neat. Michelle, too. Well, we know someone went through all the drawers in their chests because their clothes were scattered. They even looked through my makeup case. That's the only thing I keep neat enough to tell. You'd better check your stuff too, Kim."

"Has anything been stolen?" Kim asked as she rushed to her bed and pulled her suitcase out from beneath it.

"Not that we can tell yet," Susan said. "We just discovered it a few minutes ago."

Kim unzipped the lid of her case and checked inside. The package was gone! Someone must have seen her down on the trail last night, or how else would they have known to search through her cabin for the missing packet? They'd taken the sugar. This was all so crazy!

"Here's my money," Michelle said as she reached to the far corner of her bottom drawer. "It's all here, but it's in a different spot from where I put it." Her forehead wrinkled in confusion. "Why would they search our stuff, then not take the money?"

Kim knew why, but she didn't understand it. What was the big deal about a stupid package of sugar? And why drop it out of an airplane in the middle of the night?

With a firm command for the girls to lock the door behind her, Kim left the cabin to find Adam. Whatever was going on, he knew something about it. This whole thing was involving not only her now, but her girls as well, and she wanted them uninvolved immediately. She wished she'd never gone down to that clearing the other night. If anything happened to the girls. . .

She found Adam walking down the lodge steps, and she saw

how his face lit up when he saw her. He probably wouldn't feel that way much longer. "Adam, I need to talk to you."

"What's wrong?" he asked.

"I've done something you're going to hate, and we've had some repercussions."

"I'm sure it can't be that bad, Kim. What is it?"

Kim closed her eyes and bent her head. She couldn't face him right now, but he had to know. "I hiked down to the clearing last night, and I watched the drop." She heard his swift intake of breath, and her whole body went numb. Almost palpably, she could feel his disappointment. "I saw Bryson and two other people carry a big package away, and some of the contents fell out beside me."

"Did they see you?"

"I think they did, although I didn't realize it last night. I carried the packets back to the cabin with me." She paused and looked up. "Adam, it was sugar. I don't know what's going on here, but—"

He grabbed her by the shoulder. "Kim, do you still have the packets?"

"No. I'm sorry. Someone searched our cabin today while we were out. The girls discovered it. I checked the suitcase where I'd hidden the sugar—honestly, Adam, sugar?—and it was gone. I guess someone must have seen me last night." She lowered her gaze again. Just today, she'd been feeling so much better after talking with Amity, and now this. "I know I should never have gone snooping. I'm sorry, Adam. I may have endangered the girls, and I don't know what to do. I'm so sorry."

He took a deep breath and released it, looking skyward, his hand never leaving Kim's shoulder. "Did you say anything to anyone else about this?"

"No."

"Not even to the girls?"

"Especially not to the girls. You know how impetuous Carrie

is. She's liable to do—" Kim broke off, closed her eyes and shook her head. "I guess I'm just like her. I shouldn't have come here. Look what a mess I've gotten—"

His hand tightened firmly on her shoulder, and he drew her closer. "Stop it, Kim. We'll talk about that later. Right now, I've got some work to do." He bent down until he held her gaze. "Don't. Do. Anything. Else."

"I won't. I promise. I'll keep my mouth shut. But Adam. . . sugar? What on earth can sugar—"

"Kim!"

"Okay. I'm sorry."

"So you've said." He shook his head, then bent a little farther forward and kissed her forehead. "Keep your mouth shut and don't do any more snooping. Do you understand?"

"Yes. I know. I've done enough."

He hesitated, then as if he couldn't help himself, he wrapped his arms around her and drew her against his comforting chest. She let him hold her there for a long moment, and it felt wonderful. When he released her, all the self-recriminations returned. He walked her back to the cabin and waited until she went inside and locked the door behind her before he left. She watched him through the window until she could no longer see his form in the darkness.

What on earth had she done this time?

seventeen

A loud crack brought Kim staring awake. She sat up in bed like a mannequin on a string. Her nerves taut, she sat in silence until a bright flash of lightning sent sweat popping out on her skin in relief. It was an early morning thunderstorm. The resulting rain, violent and refreshing, brought a measure of comfort to her own storm-tossed emotions.

She glanced at her watch, then gasped. She had overslept again. Nothing, however, would have made her go jogging this morning with all that lightning, and she knew Adam would never dream of it. She pulled herself out of bed.

"Okay, everybody, it's time to get up." She forced a lightness to her tone and a smile to her face that she did not feel. The girls were already worried about the search through their things yesterday, especially Carrie. The girl had been unusually quiet after Kim's return last night, and Kim felt responsible. How could she do this to them?

The girls crawled out of the bed lethargically, groaning and weary eyed. The prevailing mood was one of morose despondency.

"Kim, do we have to go out in that?" Michelle complained as she sat on her bed and glared outside.

"It'll calm down in a little while," Kim consoled her. "No showers or baths this morning while there's lightning, and try to stay away from the windows. By the time we've finished breakfast, I expect the sun to be shining and the birds singing."

Carrie turned away from her baleful inspection of the dripping trees. "Some stupid bird is already out there singing."

"See? Even a bird knows it won't be long before the storm's over."

The girls stared at her from all over the room.

Kim heaved an impatient sigh. "Okay, I give up. It's a rotten day, and it'll just get rottener, and we'll all probably drown before we ever see the sun again. At this rate, we'll all drown in our self-pity."

Although the rain stopped during morning praise, a heavy mist hung about the camp as they entered the cafeteria. They brightened slightly at the aroma of frying bacon and sausage, and the sight of stacks of buttermilk pancakes on the warming table. Mrs. Morgan greeted them and gave them each a cup of hot cocoa.

"Drink up, girls. It'll warm you up and lift your spirits."

Carrie thanked her, then to everyone's surprise, invited the older woman to join them for breakfast. Mrs. Morgan took her cup of cocoa and sat with them, explaining that she had already eaten. As soon as Adam joined them, the woman started talking, regaling them with stories of past camps she'd helped with. Under cover of the woman's voice, Adam leaned close to Kim's ear.

"Did you lock your cabin door this morning?" he asked softly.

Kim nodded. "Nothing else has happened, and nothing else turned up missing. They didn't even take Michelle's money."

As Mrs. Morgan droned on, Kim noticed Carrie jerk every few moments, as if in pain. It didn't take long for Kim to realize that the other girls—at least Michelle and Joni—were kicking Carrie under the table. That wouldn't exactly encourage Carrie in Christian kindness. This was going to be a long day.

Adam scooted his chair back as soon as he'd finished. "I've got work to do, ladies. Kim, would you meet me at the lodge about thirty minutes after the girls start their first class this morning?"

"Sure."

"Oh, that's good," Mrs. Morgan said as Adam walked away. "My herbal tea is ready, and you'll have just enough time to sample it before you meet Adam." She picked up her empty cup—though how she'd had time to drink it, Kim couldn't tell. She'd been too busy talking. "I have cinnamon spice that will warm you up the rest of the day. I'll be back with it in a few minutes, Kim."

"That was stupid!" Michelle hissed at Carrie after the woman disappeared into the kitchen. "What did you invite her to sit with us for? That woman is nothing but a busybody. No one wants her around, not even the cooks."

Carrie shrugged. "I know how that feels. Now that I'm a Christian, I'm supposed to show more love to people."

"Just don't get carried away, okay?" Joni said. "Mrs. Morgan could bore a tree."

"Leave Carrie alone," Susan said. "She did the right thing. Didn't she, Kim?"

"Yes. I'm proud of you, Carrie."

"Oh sure, and now Kim gets stuck with her the rest of the morning," Michelle taunted.

Kim smiled. "I have to go see Adam, so don't worry about me."

Mrs. Morgan's return to the table a few moments later prompted Michelle and Joni to urge the others to leave early, but there was no tea. Mrs. Morgan shook her head.

"I'm sorry, Kim, but we'll have to do it another time. Adam caught me just as I was pouring. He wants you to meet him at the stables instead of the lodge. He seemed worried about one of the horses."

Kim straightened in concern. "Dozer? Is he okay?"

Mrs. Morgan spread her hands. "I don't know a thing about the animals, but I'm sure you'll find out when you get there. I'll let you get going now. See you soon, Kim." She turned and went back into the kitchen as Kim rushed out the cafeteria entrance.

No one was visible at the stables. "Adam! Dozer! What's going on out here?" Kim pursed her lips and whistled to the horse, then climbed the corral fence and scrambled down on the other side. The stables were strangely quiet. She peered into the darkened interior, and a shadow emerged on her left.

With a gasp, she swung around, then relaxed. "Dozer! You old faker. What's going on? You don't *look* sick." She reached up and scratched his ears, testing the feel of his skin, checking his eyes, and scanning his body while he nudged her and begged for a peppermint.

The click of the tack room door reached her, and she called out again. "Adam, I'm in here." She left the horse and stepped over into darker shadows near the door. "What's wrong with Dozer? I don't see—"

Something hard and heavy struck her in the side of the head. Sudden, swirling mist engulfed her before she felt the pain. The features of the room scattered, and darkness descended as a figure moved out of the shadows of the tack room. It must be Adam. . .he placed something over her face—something with a strong, caustic smell, and everything disappeared.

❧

The mist floated and eddied around Kim; one moment it would lift enough for her to see daylight, and the next moment she would feel herself being swept again into a black void. Frightening sounds echoed feverishly through her head, as if she were in a deep pit. She cried for someone to help her out, but she couldn't even hear her own voice.

A steady thump, thump, thump finally revived her numbed senses long enough for her to grasp at the consciousness and fight her way out of the mists altogether for a few moments. She forced open eyes that felt swollen and peered around the room in which she lay on a cold, hard-planked floor. Dingy, torn wallpaper covered the walls of the empty room. One tiny broken window, high on the wall, allowed some sunlight to filter through. She couldn't even think clearly enough to wonder why she was here.

The room spun around her as she tried to get up, and once more the darkness took her, though not as thoroughly as before. She still heard the thumping noise outside, and she heard voices drifting in through the door. She couldn't tell how long she lay like that, maybe minutes, maybe hours, but when she finally found the strength to pull herself back up, the sun no longer shone through the window, and the voices were now raised in argument. The vaguely familiar sound of thumping came to her again, and this time she sat up slowly, forced herself to stand, and steadied herself. For a moment, she considered calling out for someone to help her, but then she heard a voice that filled her with dread. It was Bryson.

"We'll at least have to keep her overnight, or she'll blow the whole deal," his voice came through the door.

Someone else spoke briefly, and Kim recognized the feminine tones of Priscilla Waters, all the soft, seductive sweetness gone from her voice. Kim couldn't tell what she said.

Bryson spoke again. "It makes no difference to me; it would be stupid to kill her just for that. Besides, they'll never find us where we're headed."

Kim stiffened. Kill her! They were talking about killing her the way most people would talk about the price of tomatoes! That couldn't have been Adam at the stables. But hadn't he been the one to tell Mrs. Morgan. . .?

She couldn't just wait around for them to decide what to do with her. She glanced at the window and once again heard the thumping sound. If they were holding her prisoner, they had probably posted a guard outside, but she'd check and see.

With silence foremost in her mind, she stole over to the opening. She peered outside, then caught her breath in surprise at the beautiful, powerful sight of Dozer grazing near the window, stomping the soft, muddy ground with his huge feet—thus the thumping sound.

"Thank You, Lord," Kim whispered. "Help me get out of here, please!" She grasped the edge of a piece of broken glass and worked it gently back and forth. The wood was rotting, and the pane must have been loose already because the large piece of glass slipped out easily. With as much silence as she could muster, she pulled out the rest of the pieces and stuck her head outside, praying that the huge horse would wait for her—and praying that she could fit through the tiny opening.

She took a steadying breath, stretched her arms through the opening, and pulled herself up and halfway through. The wood scraped her skin and dug into her ribs. The voices stopped in the other room for a moment, and she froze. Were they coming to get her?

With a desperate thrust, she forced herself farther out, lost her balance, and fell several feet, headfirst, into the mud below. Ugh!

She pulled herself upright, then nearly cried out in fright when a heavy shadow loomed over her. It was Dozer, his big, curious eyes next to hers, his long nose checking out the mud on her jeans. She hugged him quickly, then pulled herself up.

"Dozer, if you came to rescue me," she whispered, "just stand still while I get on you."

She guided the willing horse over to a tall tree stump, used his bulk to boost herself onto the stump, then grabbed a handful of his long mane. A door slammed at the other side of the house. Dozer snorted and stepped sideways, pulling Kim with him.

She darted a terrified glance toward the house. Nothing stirred. "Dozer, if you love me, please come back here and be still." She urged him once again to the stump. This time he stood for her as she swung her leg over his back and slipped on.

Someone shouted from the right side of the house. Dozer snorted, and Kim turned to see Bryson and Priscilla running toward her.

"Catch her!" Priscilla shrieked. "Knock her off or drag her off; just catch her!"

Kim dug her heels into Dozer's sides and grasped his mane tightly. "Go, Dozer! Go!"

Bryson lunged for her as Priscilla stopped running and turned toward the house. Dozer leaped forward, the powerful legs thrusting horse and rider away, out of Bryson's grasp and into the woods, where pine branches slapped and stung Kim's face and arms.

She dared to look back and gasped when she saw Bryson still coming after her through the woods. He ran swiftly, his legs pumping like those of a track star, his breath coming loud and angry as he dodged the trees.

"Hurry, Dozer, faster!" Kim screamed. She hugged herself to the horse, lying nearly flat against his neck, feeling his powerful muscles straining beneath her body.

A loud boom jerked her upright in shock, just as she felt a violent, searing pain in her left side, just below the rib cage. The force of it wrenched her from the galloping horse as if someone had pushed her. Dozer thundered on through the trees and out of sight as Kim lay on the soft forest floor, unable to move from the sudden shock of the fall.

"You fool!" came Bryson's voice through the trees. "Are you crazy? What if someone heard that? Are you trying to add murder to your list of crimes?" His harsh voice grew louder as he drew near and stepped into the tiny clearing where Kim had fallen. He rushed to her side and knelt down.

She shuddered and jerked away from him as he reached out toward her, but the movement sent a shaft of pain through her side and she cried out in pain. Priscilla followed him, a dark gray handgun in her right hand.

"Be quiet. Lie still," Bryson said with surprising gentleness. "Where did it hit you?" He searched for and found the wound in Kim's left side, probed it until she cried out again, then shot an angry glare back at Priscilla. "If you're lucky, we might be able to get her back to the cabin and stanch the flow of blood."

The woman's unperturbed gaze rested on Kim. "Why not just finish the job now, Bryson?"

Kim caught her breath and felt Bryson's hand tighten over her arm. "Because I'm not a murderer."

Priscilla raised an eyebrow. "She's not going to send me to prison."

"And I'm not going to prison for murder," Bryson shot back harshly. He lifted Kim gently into his arms and carried her through the forest, back toward the dilapidated cabin, ignoring the blond-haired woman who followed closely behind and kept a steady, deadly gaze locked on Kim.

They walked into the front room of the old shack, and as Bryson lay Kim down onto a moth-eaten couch, she grew aware, through the haze of pain, that another person occupied the house. She smelled smoke, and she turned in the shadowed dimness to see the familiar face of Mrs. Morgan sitting in a straight-backed chair across the room. The woman pulled a cigarette from her lips and blew a puff of haze that thickened the atmosphere.

Kim felt tears fill her eyes as dizziness threatened once more to take her. "Mrs. Morgan? Why? What are you—?"

"Get some blankets," Bryson snapped. "She's going into shock." The sound of his voice drifted. "And some towels. She's still blee—" The voice, and the room, disappeared.

Sometime later—Kim had no idea how long—a stinging pain in her side brought her back to lethargic consciousness. She opened her eyes to find Bryson packing her wound with strips of white cloth. Kim tried to pull away, but Bryson held her more firmly.

"Hold still. This is helping," he said.

Kim looked up to find Priscilla's glossed lips curving into a satisfied smile. "You might as well give it up. I hear Robert's car coming, and you know what he'll say."

Mrs. Morgan got up from her chair and walked over to the window, where evening dusk had come early with the overcast sky. "It's him, all right."

Bryson ignored them both and continued working over Kim. He glanced into Kim's eyes briefly and, to her surprise, lay a hand on her arm before rising to face whoever was coming through the door.

Kim looked up and could not contain a cry of shock when she saw the face of their interim director, Mr. Waters. No! It couldn't be.

With a cold, hard stare at her, he stalked into the room. His eyes narrowed at Priscilla. "What's she doing here?"

"Where else were we supposed to take her?"

"I don't care, but not here! You were supposed to get rid of her."

"I tried to, but Bryson just wants to keep her overnight and send her running back to camp tomorrow."

Waters turned his angry glare on Bryson. "Stupid! She would identify us."

"She almost escaped already," Priscilla snapped. "Bryson left the door to the bedroom closed, and she climbed out the window."

"How she fit through that tiny hole, I couldn't tell," Mrs. Morgan said. "I didn't think anything but a squirrel could fit—"

"Why is she bleeding?" Waters asked.

"I shot her," Priscilla said.

"You have a lousy aim. Okay, everyone, get your dark clothes on and let's get going. Our pickup time is earlier than we'd expected."

"What about her?" Priscilla nodded toward Kim.

"Kill her."

Kim gasped. She saw Bryson back toward her and spread his arms out in front of her protectively.

"What's wrong, Matt?" Priscilla asked with a smile. "Don't have the stomach for it?"

"Have you all gone crazy?"

"Just tie her up and leave her," Mrs. Morgan said. "We'll be long gone after the last drop, and no one knows where—"

"Shut up!" Waters casually placed his hand into the right pocket of his denim jacket. "Why have you suddenly gone soft on us, Matt?"

"I'm not a killer."

"Oh? Not a killer, just a drug runner? You pretend to protect that camp full of delinquent brats from people like yourself."

"What's your real name, Robert?" Bryson asked suddenly. "I've been curious ever since you arrived at camp, pretending to be the man they interviewed over the phone."

"You don't need to worry about that." Robert took a step closer, and his eyes narrowed. "You've suddenly developed another problem. Have you been playing spy games with the wrong people?"

Bryson said nothing. Kim thought about Adam and knew suddenly that Waters was telling the truth. Bryson must be working with Adam to catch this ring of criminals, and the man who was supposed to be interim director never made it to camp. Everything fell into place. Unfortunately, Priscilla picked up on it too.

"You're right, Robert. Patterson's in on it. I've seen them with their heads together too many times."

"And what about the sugar your people substituted for the real stuff?" Waters demanded.

"What are you talking about?"

"You were supposed to check each delivery." Waters smiled a wicked smile as he stepped closer to Bryson. "You checked, all right, and you knew about the substitution. You just never said anything about it. If Priscilla hadn't recognized that brat in Miss Bryant's cabin"—he shot Kim a baleful glare—"and discovered the sugar under that bed, we wouldn't have caught you. Trying to pull a sting operation? How stupid do you think I am? And what about Doss Carpenter?"

Kim suppressed another gasp, and her sudden expression of

surprise drew Priscilla's attention. The woman reached toward the gun she had placed on the edge of a scarred coffee table.

"No!" Bryson snapped. He stepped forward to grab the gun, but Waters pulled his own gun out of his pocket and fired.

Bryson grunted and stumbled against the table, knocking it over. The gun fell onto the floor.

Waters aimed at Kim. Bryson shouted and kicked the weapon away as Kim cried out and tried to scramble off the couch. Priscilla dove for her gun and grasped it in both hands, rolling toward the other side of the room. Shouts came from outside, and Priscilla aimed just as the front door burst open like an explosion, with Adam tumbling in behind it.

"Adam, look out!" Kim screamed.

Bryson lunged toward Priscilla as three uniformed police officers followed Adam into the room. The sound of another shot rang through the small room, and Priscilla cried out in agony as one of the policemen helped Adam subdue Waters. The other two officers rushed to Priscilla, whose shoulder was splashed with blood. Mrs. Morgan jumped up from her chair and ran toward the open door, but she cried out in fear and came stumbling back inside, followed by a huge menacing form. Dozer.

eighteen

Kim awakened to find herself in a private hospital room and the sun shining through opened blinds. She didn't feel any pain in her left side until she tried to move. Then she grimaced and caught her breath.

She heard water pouring and turned to find Adam on the left side of her bed, filling a glass with water from a pitcher. "You need to drink this," he said with a smile as he placed the glass onto the bedside stand. "If it leaks out, it means they didn't give you enough stitches."

She smiled in spite of the continuing ache. At the sight of her smile, he leaned over and, without invitation, kissed her on the forehead.

"Where are we?"

"Branson. You don't have any idea how happy I was to see you alive last night in that shack." His eyes grew serious.

"You couldn't have been as relieved as I was," Kim said. "Although I was terrified you were going to be shot as soon as you came barreling through the door."

His eyes held her for a long moment, until she closed her own and turned away. "I almost got you killed, Adam. You and Bryson both. I'm sorry. I can never forgive myself for that."

"Bryson holds no grudges against you, Kim. They took the bullet out of his arm last night, and he's doing fine. You just got a graze, so you have twenty-five stitches altogether. No vital structures have been touched, and you're as strong as an ox, so you'll heal. You'll probably go home today. You were really out of it last night, with the pain medication."

"How about you?"

He frowned at her. "I didn't get hurt."

161

"You haven't said if you forgive me or not."

He smiled, but when he saw the expression of concern on her face, the smile turned gentle. "It matters to you?"

"Of course it matters! You were mad at me for five years. I don't want it to become a habit."

"I don't have to forgive you, Kim. I wasn't mad at you to begin with."

She returned his smile, then she sobered. "You saved our lives. They were getting ready to shoot me, and Bryson blew his cover trying to protect me."

"Dozer was the one who saved you, Kim. He came running into camp yesterday with blood and drying mud on his left flank, no bridle or saddle. I called the police when no one could find you or Bryson, and when we saw the direction Dozer headed back out of camp, we knew where to look. Dozer beat us there."

"They were running drugs, weren't they?"

"Cocaine."

"But the sugar—"

"The Drug Enforcement Agency has been trying to catch this ring for a long time, and the ones you met are only a small fraction of the group. They've already rounded up others down the line. One overexuberant agent grabbed the drug shipment too soon, and the sugar was the result of a heroic effort to keep the delivery on time and out of suspicion."

"Mr. Waters said something about one of my campers being involved."

"Carrie."

Kim nodded. She knew Carrie had been in trouble with the police.

"She recognized Priscilla Waters and Doss Carpenter because she worked with them a couple of times, just before she was taken into custody for possession. She told me about Priscilla and so did Doss."

"He was involved too?" Kim asked.

"Yes. He told me all about it the night I followed him and Carrie into Branson. He got involved with Priscilla while he was still in medical school. She discovered he was having financial problems and that he might have to quit before he graduated. She introduced him to a lucrative alternative. He told me he was desperate enough to consider it, but as soon as they asked him to start smuggling, he had second thoughts and tried to back out. Priscilla wouldn't let him. When he finally graduated and moved to Branson to get away from the whole mess, she followed him and threatened that if he didn't cooperate, she'd ruin his career. That woman has a lot of power. That power ultimately caused the wreck that injured the previously scheduled camp doctor."

"So that's how Doss got the job here," Kim said. "Bryson mentioned something about the camp interim director being an imposter."

"He was. Remember that I mentioned it to you one day? The director didn't seem like the same man I'd interviewed over the telephone. He wasn't. The director I interviewed wasn't Priscilla's brother, either, although she spread word that he was. It was coincidence that they shared the last name, and Priscilla made the most of it. I think they're going to find, when they investigate that woman further, that she made the most of every situation."

In spite of what Kim knew about Doss now, she still felt a keen sense of disappointment at his involvement with the drug ring. "What happened to the real Mr. Waters?"

"I just found out this morning that his car was hijacked. The Feds found him safe and alive out in a wilderness cabin in Arkansas and have kept him under protective custody until this operation could be wrapped up. Apparently the people Priscilla hires to do her dirty work aren't as bloodthirsty as she is."

"This explains why Carrie was so afraid of Doss at first. How does Mrs. Morgan fit into all this?" Kim asked. "I was so shocked to see her at that cabin, but I shouldn't have been. She was the one who told me to go to the stables to meet you."

Adam took a deep breath and let it out slowly. "Morgan is a newcomer. When they questioned her, I heard her blaming Robert Waters for everything and crying because she couldn't make a living on her pension, couldn't get disability, and she had a bad back. They used her as a gofer."

"What's going to happen to her?"

"I don't know, Kim. At least partly because of her, you're in the hospital and Bryson's got a hole in his arm." Adam glanced at his watch. "Speaking of Bryson, I've got to go to a meeting with him and some men from Washington, D.C. It seems Bryson is one of the DEA's best agents."

"Adam, please thank Bryson for me. And tell him how sorry I am for nearly getting him killed. Oh, and Adam," she whispered conspiratorially, "the Appalachian Trail is a much *safer* adventure."

Adam smiled sheepishly. "Anyway, Mom and Dad will be here soon, and they'll stay with you until you're checked out. Then you're going home with them to Eureka Springs."

"Oh yeah?"

"Yes. No arguments, or I'll ask the doctor to keep you here for another twenty-four hours."

Kim laid her head back on her pillow. "I don't suppose I can go back to camp, can I?"

"No. I want you to recuperate."

"That won't take four more weeks."

"We have another counselor coming to take your place this afternoon." He leaned forward and kissed her forehead again, then glanced at his watch once more. "I'll be seeing you soon. Just get well."

❧

Kim did as she was told, and a little more. That afternoon she arranged for Pam to drive her car to the Pattersons'. She would rest and recuperate, as Adam had said, but she would not stay in Eureka Springs forever. At the Pattersons' home in Eureka Springs, Kim did nothing to reinjure herself. She ate what Kate gave her to eat, caught up with the past five years with Kate and John, and even visited with Amity and Titus King when they came by to see her on Tuesday evening.

By Wednesday morning, she awakened to find herself feeling stronger and suffering very little pain—at least not physically. Mentally, she couldn't stop the guilt that ate at her and the knowledge that Adam had easily placed someone else with the girls whom she had come to love in the past two weeks. They were probably getting along great without her. They probably didn't even miss her. By noon, she was dressed and ready to go home.

"I wish you'd rethink this," John said as he and Kate walked Kim to her car. "I think you need a little more time to heal. Besides, you don't have to go back to work yet."

"And Adam's due to arrive anytime," Kate added. "He'll be so disappointed if you're not here."

"He won't be disappointed; he'll be mad that I didn't follow his orders." Kim forced a smile. "He'll live."

Kate raised a motherly brow. "Kimberly Bryant, you're just as bullheaded as you ever were."

The words stung more than they were meant to. Kate was right. Kim felt as if she hadn't changed at all these past five years, that she hadn't learned a thing, hadn't matured. No wonder Adam had so quickly found a replacement for her at the camp. She truly was a horrible example for young, impressionable girls to follow.

"I know, Kate. I'm sorry." She hugged her foster parents, promised to call them as soon as she arrived home, and climbed into her car. Before she could start the engine and pull away, however, another car pulled in front of her on the curb, facing the wrong direction.

Kim glanced up in surprise to find Adam behind the steering wheel. She waved at him, smiling sheepishly. He did not wave back, nor did he return her smile.

He got out of the car and came over to lean next to her open window. "Where do you think you're going?"

Her smile turned to a grimace. "Oh great," she muttered. "I'm going to get the big brother act again." At the same time, she could not suppress the surge of joy she felt at seeing him.

At her words, he sighed and shook his head. "Scoot over, Kim," he said, opening her car door. "I don't want you to move any more than necessary."

"What do you mean, scoot over? It's my car."

"But I'm not good at giving directions, and I want to show you something."

She frowned at him. For a moment, he returned her frown, then he relented and took on an expression of sweet entreaty.

"Please, Kim? I drove all the way down here just to talk to you."

"About what?"

"About us." He turned to his parents, who continued to stand on the front lawn, watching the exchange with avid interest. "We'll be back before long."

Kate shot him an understanding smile. "Take your time, you two. You've got a lot of catching up to do."

Kim finally scooted across the bench seat of her car, allowing Adam to slip behind the wheel. "What is it you want to show me?" she asked as he started the engine and pulled out onto the street.

"You'll see."

She sat for several minutes in silence as he maneuvered through the busy downtown section of Eureka Springs, where tourists jaywalked as a matter of habit on the narrow winding road. They headed out toward the edge of town. She stared at all the new buildings and shopping centers that had been built in the five years since she'd left. Her hometown didn't look the same.

"A lot has changed," she said quietly.

"We'll have to come back and explore when you're feeling better."

"I'd like that. Adam, Kate said something a while ago that made me realize something. A lot has changed, but in some ways I haven't. I'm still the same bullheaded troublemaker I've always been. After five years, that hasn't changed."

He glanced sideways at her. "I know."

She bent her head and looked at her hands. That hurt.

He reached across with one hand and covered hers. "Kim," he said gently, "you may need to learn more prudence, but you do not need to change the person you are. You're strong-willed and full of vibrance and curiosity." About a mile past the edge of town, he turned onto a narrow paved lane, and cruised slowly beneath a deep canopy of trees. "I don't think you've ever been here," he said.

She looked around them. "No. Where are we going?"

"You know that school Titus and Amity are planning to build?" As he spoke, they drove down a long hillside and into a grassy clearing. A small, simple church building sat at one end of the hollow, and a bulldozer sat at the other, where the foundation for a much larger building was being dug deeply into the side of a hill.

"This is the place?" Kim asked with a sudden smile. "It's beautiful!"

He parked the car, then turned to look at Kim. "That church is where they were married last year."

"Very picturesque."

"So is their marriage." Adam leaned back and turned toward Kim, resting his left forearm across the steering wheel. "They have a strong, good marriage, and they're more in love than they were on their honeymoon. I've never seen Titus happier. That's what happens when two people are put together by God and allow Him to develop their relationship in His will."

Kim held his steady gaze for a moment, then looked away.

She dared not even think about the hope that his words and actions gave her. How could she?

"Did you and Amity have a good visit Sunday?" he asked.

"Yes, we did."

He reached forward and raised Kim's chin until she was forced to look at him again. "Did it soak in?"

"What?"

"She told you about her previous marriage, didn't she?"

"Yes. Adam, what are you talking about?"

He released her and leaned back again, closing his eyes and shaking his head. "I'm doing this all wrong, I know. It's just that I've never done it before, and I hope I never have to do it again."

"What are you doing?"

He remained with his eyes closed. "Proposing. Marriage. To you."

Kim's mouth dropped open and she gasped. "To me? Why on earth would you want to marry me? I've caused you nothing but trouble for the past five years, and the trend doesn't seem to have changed in the past two weeks. I almost got you and Bryson killed—"

"—and yourself. Don't forget that."

"Thank you very much," she said through gritted teeth. "And I might even have put my campers in danger. And—"

"And you led Carrie to Christ. And your influence helped lead Doss to Christ." His head came up and he looked at her again.

"And you were so eager to get me out of camp that you immediately replaced me with another counselor."

"I was eager to get you healed. Since I know how headstrong you are, I knew better than to let you come back to camp too soon because you wouldn't allow yourself time to rest."

"Still pulling the big brother act with me, aren't you?"

"No, Kim, I'm not!" He glared at her. "What I'm doing is

acting like a man in love, because I am, and I think I've loved you all my life—all our lives. I knew I'd missed you, but I never realized how much until I saw you, and started spending time with you again. Kim, I can't lose you again. I just can't do that. You can be the most stubborn, willful, and infuriating person in the four-state area, but I've had my whole life thus far to get used to that." He stopped, as if realizing that his voice carried all the way across the clearing. "And you're also the most fun, fascinating person in the world to me. You stretch my spirit, my emotions, my intellect—weak as that may be at times." He finished softly, "I can't imagine life with anyone else."

Kim couldn't suppress a smile. "You can be romantic when the mood strikes, can't you?"

He didn't even blush. "Will you marry me?"

"How do you know I love you?"

"Because I see it in your eyes every time you look at me. I feel it every time you touch me. I also know why you've been avoiding this conversation, and I think that shows your love more fully than anything else—misguided, but sincere. You wanted what you thought was best for me, and you did not feel you could be. You'll just have to accept the fact that you're wrong about—"

"Okay."

"What?"

The laughter hurt her side, but she couldn't help it. "Yes, Adam."

"Yes, what?"

"Yes, I'll marry you."

He stared at her. "You mean it?"

Her smile broadened. "I love you, Adam. It's a love God placed in my heart, and it won't go away. My. . .teenage marriage was not for love, it was out of fear, and rebellion, and lack of dependence on God. I felt unworthy of someone like you, and maybe I always will, but you were right to sic Amity on me. I've been thinking about what she said. If God has decided to give me a second chance at real happiness, who am I to turn Him down? In my opinion, that would be a sin."

"So you're saying that if you didn't marry me you'd be sinning?"

"That's the way I see it."

A smile lit his eyes, and he reached for her and drew her into his arms. "I like the way you see things, Kimberly Bryant."

A Letter To Our Readers

Dear Reader:

In order that we might better contribute to your reading enjoyment, we would appreciate your taking a few minutes to respond to the following questions. We welcome your comments and read each form and letter we receive. When completed, please return to the following:

Rebecca Germany, Fiction Editor
Heartsong Presents
PO Box 719
Uhrichsville, Ohio 44683

1. Did you enjoy reading *Ozark Sunrise?*
   ☐ Very much. I would like to see more books by this author!
   ☐ Moderately
   I would have enjoyed it more if _____
   _____
   _____

2. Are you a member of **Heartsong Presents**? Yes ☐ No ☐
   If no, where did you purchase this book?_____
   _____

3. How would you rate, on a scale from 1 (poor) to 5 (superior), the cover design?_____

4. On a scale from 1 (poor) to 10 (superior), please rate the following elements.

   _____ Heroine   _____ Plot

   _____ Hero   _____ Inspirational theme

   _____ Setting   _____ Secondary characters

5. These characters were special because_____

   _____

   _____

6. How has this book inspired your life?_____

   _____

   _____

7. What settings would you like to see covered in future
   Heartsong Presents books?_____

   _____

   _____

8. What are some inspirational themes you would like to see
   treated in future books?_____

   _____

   _____

9. Would you be interested in reading other **Heartsong
   Presents** titles?   Yes ☐   No ☐

10. Please check your age range:
    ☐ Under 18   ☐ 18-24   ☐ 25-34
    ☐ 35-45   ☐ 46-55   ☐ Over 55

11. How many hours per week do you read?_____

Name _____

Occupation _____

Address _____

City _____ State _____ Zip _____

This heartwarming collection of short stories is perfect

for "want to" readers—those big on reading but short on time. From the story of an engaged couple looking for common ground amongst their dissimilarities to the account of a single mother's thoughts as her daughter desires to meet the father who left them, this collection of inspirational short stories is sometimes light-hearted, sometimes humorous, and often poignant. Focusing on the joys and heartaches of love—romantic love, love for family members, love between friends, even the love of an elderly gentleman for his pets—*Short Stories for Long Rainy Days* will bring gentle smiles, soft chuckles, and even a few tears as readers experience the manifold facets of love. 224 pages, Hardbound, 5 x 7

♥ ♥ ♥ ♥ ♥ ♥ ♥ ♥ ♥ ❤ ♥ ♥ ♥ ♥ ♥ ♥ ♥ ♥ ♥

♥ ♥ ♥ ♥ ♥ ♥ ♥ ♥ ♥ ❤ ♥ ♥ ♥ ♥ ♥ ♥ ♥ ♥ ♥

·······Presents·······

Great Inspirational Romance at a Great Price!

Heartsong Presents books are inspirational romances in contemporary and historical settings, designed to give you an enjoyable, spirit-lifting reading experience. You can choose wonderfully written titles from some of today's best authors like Veda Boyd Jones, Yvonne Lehman, Tracie Peterson, Debra White Smith, and many others.

When ordering quantities less than twelve, above titles are $2.95 each.
Not all titles may be available at time of order.

SEND TO: **Heartsong Presents** Reader's Service
P.O. Box 719, Uhrichsville, Ohio 44683

Please send me the items checked above. I am enclosing $_____
(please add $1.00 to cover postage per order. OH add 6.25% tax. NJ add 6%.). Send check or money order, no cash or C.O.D.s, please.
To place a credit card order, call 1-800-847-8270.

NAME _____

ADDRESS _____

CITY/STATE _____ ZIP _____

HPS 8-99

Heart♥ng Presents
Love Stories Are Rated G!

That's for godly, gratifying, and of course, great! If you love a thrilling love story, but don't appreciate the sordidness of some popular paperback romances, **Heartsong Presents** is for you. In fact, **Heartsong Presents** is the *only inspirational romance book club*, the only one featuring love stories where Christian faith is the primary ingredient in a marriage relationship.

Sign up today to receive your first set of four, never before published Christian romances. Send no money now; you will receive a bill with the first shipment. You may cancel at any time without obligation, and if you aren't completely satisfied with any selection, you may return the books for an immediate refund!

Imagine. . .four new romances every four weeks—two historical, two contemporary—with men and women like you who long to meet the one God has chosen as the love of their lives. . .all for the low price of $9.97 postpaid.

To join, simply complete the coupon below and mail to the address provided. **Heartsong Presents** romances are rated G for another reason: They'll arrive *Godspeed!*